Hidden
&
Other Stories

Victoria Taylor Roberts

Copyright © Victoria Taylor Roberts 2010

Cover design by Victoria Taylor Roberts

All rights reserved. No part of this publication may be reproduced, stored in a retrieval system, or transmitted in any form or by any means, electronic, mechanical, photocopy, recording or otherwise, without prior written permission of the copyright owner. Nor can it be circulated in any form of binding or cover other than that in which it is published and without similar condition including this condition being imposed on a subsequent purchaser.

British Library Cataloguing in Publication Data.
A catalogue record for this book is available from the British Library.

ISBN 9798712237913

For Brian and Tess

Contents

1. A Toast

9. Hidden

18. Raffle Boy

35. A Day Out

45. Her Last Words

46. License to Drive

81. Hotel Room

83. Evensong

89. Just a Rose

91. Lady on a Train

94. The Smell of Rain

105. The Vase

114. A Quick Lunch

123. To the New Year

A Toast

Leaning against the cooker, Derek Thompson reached into the cupboard above it and pulled out an unopened bottle of Rioja. Dusting it down with a tea towel, he paused to read the label's description, 'a rich nutty flavour with spicy undertones' - the thought pleased him. He imagined a taste similar to mulled wine and congratulated himself for having unwittingly chosen one so appropriate. The bottle felt reassuringly heavy in his hands and Derek was pleasantly surprised to discover the smooth emerald glass was slightly warm.

The kitchen, which faced north, overlooking a small and rather scruffy communal garden, was bitterly cold at this time of year and, Derek noted, sniffing the air disdainfully, smelled faintly of damp. Still, he'd at least chosen a good place to store his wine.

Derek rarely kept alcohol at home. He wasn't a drinker of spirits (aside from the odd sociable whisky) and his taste for lager had faded with his growing older and less inclined to join his young colleagues at the office for the customary Friday night booze-ups. Most of them thirty years his junior, they were a rowdy bunch of lads whose manners were more that of builders than book keepers; always eyeing up the girls and bragging in their thick London accents about their closing time fumbles the week before. Derek found it difficult to keep up with their ballistic jibes and pilfered sketch show humour. These were men of a different generation, always talking of analysing the competition or gaining experience before setting up their own consultancies. Self-employment was something that had never occurred to Derek. He had felt sincerely grateful to secure his first job so soon after passing his accountancy exams (having failed them once previously) and that sense of gratitude and humility had stayed with him, quelling any curiosity of those exploits that involved even the slightest risk or uncertainty. The young men's banter made him feel unfashionable and he avoided any input into the conversations: Derek didn't feel he had anything to contribute to their talk of grand schemes and financial freedom. As the bold and ambitious moved on, fresh new faces appeared; always young, always eager, they brought new humour, new stories of sexual prowess, thus saving the evolving clan from ever having to mature. Derek alone had grown old amongst them, sitting on the periphery of office banter, smiling on cue at the barrage of bad jokes and politely signing leaving cards when asked to. It did not seem too large a price to pay for consistency.

He had worked at the same small accountancy firm for eighteen years. It was a cramped, second story office in Wells street, close to Oxford Circus. Having not had a coat of paint in almost a decade, it was, one had to admit, extremely grubby, but he was comfortable there – fond, even, of its scruffiness and the cheap, dusty wildlife prints that adorned its Magnolia walls. Derek's desk was near the window. This was considered an honoured position as, although there were two sash windows facing the street, only the one beside his desk actually opened. His previous boss Alan, who Derek remembered as being a kind man with ginger hair and a pretty wife, had moved him there several years earlier in recognition of his seniority. It was a kind gesture, meant to compensate Derek for the refusal of his request to be moved into the spare office. The company had been using it as a storeroom since the seventies. Most of the dusty cabinets were half empty and Derek thought that, once tidied, the room could be put to good use. Having, by then, worked with the company for nearly thirteen years, Derek took it for granted that his proposal would be accepted. In retrospect, perhaps he'd acted naively, but at the time it had seemed a sensible solution considering how crowded the main office had become. It was two weeks before management responded. Derek couldn't understand why they had refused him - but he didn't question it; instead he had simply smiled and thanked Alan when he offered him the desk by the window; and quietly, without ceremony, moved his belongings from one set of drawers to the other.

Management's decision had turned out to be fortuitous. The next summer had been a hot one and Derek had grown to love being by the window, thankful not to be stuck at the back of the dark and stuffy office. In moments of idleness, he would gaze down at the busy side street, studying the figures that jostled for space on its narrow concrete pavements. Through the day, his co-workers would stand by his desk, exchanging pleasantries whilst peering out of the open window for girls in short skirts to leer at. The more brazen would rest their palms on the sill and, poking their upper bodies through the frame, call out to their prey. Rarely did they get a response, but that didn't seem to daunt them. Derek admired the young men's fearlessness. It did not even occur to them that they offered themselves up for rejection time and time again. They approached women as nonchalantly as they would a friendly game of football: a possible goal to score and brag about later.

Derek was close to retirement now; another five years and his time would be his own. Normally a practical man who'd always taken pleasure in planning the finer details of his life, Derek had not paused to contemplate what lay ahead of him once the perennial routine of Monday to Friday came to an end.

It was a train of thought he had chosen not to pursue; time would come soon enough when it was all Derek would have to think about. He knew this and studied avoidance as diligently as he did the pages of numbers that were placed before him each morning. The fact that they continued to appear every day, begging his competent assistance, waiting impatiently to be stamped and processed was, to Derek, enough for now.

There was a half eaten turkey sandwich in the fridge and he took that and the glass of wine he had poured into the sitting room. Even in darkness he moved deftly between the small piles of books that littered the room and ignoring the two armchairs sat himself at his desk beneath the window. At its corner an office lamp perched like a mechanical arm, poised as if to unfurl at any moment. He switched it on and blinked involuntarily as its spotlight flooded the desk, framing the wine and sandwich like a drab still life painting. Moving them to one side, Derek opened the drawer to his left and took out a black, pocket-sized diary with the year embossed in gold italics on the cover. There was a suit jacket hanging neatly over the chair and he reached behind him and into the inside breast pocket, pulling out a diary identical to the one on the desk. Placing the diaries side by side in front of him Derek took a couple of sips of wine and a bite of his sandwich and then, contemplating the cover of the older, scuffed pocket book, traced the imprint of its long faded number with his finger. Pressing the diary open at the address section near the back, he turned to its un-battered twin and studied the cover appraisingly - enjoying the faint animal odour that emanated from it. As he opened it, the book's spine cracked, its virgin leather creaking in protest like stressed wood. Derek was reminded of the snow-covered trees he'd passed that morning whilst taking his constitutional. Lining the parks main parade, they had stood like battle worn soldiers, their over-burdened branches twisted by age and wet weather. It had been very windy that day and as each gust tore through them, the row of oaks had groaned in unison, their shudders causing each to shed a little more of its white, wintry veneer. How glorious they had looked to Derek. And now the sound of the crisp new chronicle in his hands - and what it epitomized, gave him a momentary thrill.

Opening the right hand drawer Derek took care to select a pen that he knew wouldn't splodge and spoil the uniform effect of his tight, angular writing. He turned to the back of the diary and flicked through its gilded pages until he found the section reserved for addresses and telephone numbers. With both books open before him he paused for a moment, then picked up the pen and began to copy from one diary to another. It was important that he wrote neatly and clearly and remembered to categorize the entries for easy reference; diaries became such messy things when not kept properly. Each year Derek would read through the list and weed those he felt were redundant. These usually consisted of contact names at companies he'd dealt with briefly (plumbers, belligerent pension advisers and such). Last year he'd found himself scrubbing out the names of old friends; putting a line through old school pal Tom had been the hardest. His dear friend Tom Hanson had died of a heart attack in '99. Sixty-three and seemingly full of life, he had just keeled over in the garden one Sunday morning whilst planting Begonias. Derek had received a tearful call from Missy, Tom's wife. Poor thing, she had rung every number in Tom's pocket book, rounding up as many as she could of his old mates for the funeral.

Derek had run into Jim Staunton at the graveside. He looked well and although sad for the loss of their friend, seemed quite chirpy overall. This was not surprising, since he informed Derek that he was now living in Portugal and doing little more than soaking up the sun from the comfort of a Lilo in the middle of his swimming pool. Derek didn't resent it: Jim had been the most industrious of all of them, working like a Trojan for as long as Derek could remember. No, Jim certainly deserved his time in the sun. Derek reached for his wine. 'Good for him' he thought and lifted his glass in a silent toast to old friends. He scanned the list again. Unfortunately, as they'd said their goodbyes after the funeral, Jim had forgotten to give Derek his address. 'No matter' he thought, Jim knew where to find him. Derek had bought the flat in Camden Square - many years before its discovery by the middle class families that now dominated its Georgian terraces. He'd got it for a good price and had been very happy there. There was only one bedroom and it wasn't very large, but within minutes of walking into it and seeing the bay window and its view of the square's communal garden, he had decided that it suited him perfectly and had put in an offer an hour later. His married friends had teased him about his 'bachelor pad', envious of what they considered freedom. This pleased Derek and he didn't discourage their jibes, liking the persona it gave him. What Derek never confided was that he would have very happily shared the space with someone – had there been someone who'd wanted to share it with him. Of course he'd had lovers and one or two of the relationships had been quite serious. But somehow, their interest always seemed to fade before the question of marriage came up. Now, at sixty, it seemed unlikely that it would. When Derek was in his forties, Jim's wife, Mel (short for Emmeline) would regularly invite him to dinner, insisting that he be introduced to every female co-worker and friend she possessed. Tactlessly feigning nonchalance she would parade the faded debutantes before him week after week, constructing some of the most painfully embarrassing scenes of Derek's life. But he was fond of her - and grateful to her for wanting him to be happy. It hadn't been that bad he supposed. One of the women, Moira her name was, had been very pleasant company indeed – they'd even dated once or twice (although nothing ever came of it). He smiled now at the ingenuous kindness that had been, then, so torturous. Jim and Tom had found the whole thing hilarious of course; his old school pals happy to, once again, make Derek the butt of their jokes. It had never occurred to either of them that he might remain alone. It had never occurred to Derek either.

Above the cold fireplace, on a mantle in front of the mirror, stood a carriage clock doubling as a bookend for an untidy row of condensed novels. All were identically bound with Reader's Digest printed on each spine and pale yellow corners of hidden post-it notes peeked out from some, giving them the appearance of being well read. As the minute hand hit twelve and slipped into the shadow of the hand that marked the hour, the clock came to life and rang out, defiantly filling the dim, muted room and jerking Derek from his reverie.

"Damn thing" he said softly and lifted the glass to his lips.

It was only once the entries had been sorted into lists of current and non-current and the latter copied into the stiff little book that was to be his new companion; that Derek paused. Last on the list was his brother's name, Daniel. He scribed the 'D' slowly, in a copperplate fashion, letting his pen trail into the next letter, as he did when writing his own name.

"It's been a long time little brother" he murmured and smiled fondly at the mental image of that gawky little boy who would follow him home from school each day, prattling on in the inane manner at which young children are so adept. As a toddler Daniel had adored him. It was the closest Derek had ever come to being anybody's hero. Daniel grew up to be an incredibly inquisitive and mischievous child, quickly absorbing the world around him and measuring himself against others with arrogant certainty. Visiting relatives would click their tongues in disapproval when they spoke of 'that wicked boy's exploits' and yet, with smiles as broad as melon slices, they would throw their arms around him when he entered the room, their soft cheeks flushed with genuine affection. It was obvious to Derek then that his brother had outgrown him. Sixteen years old and used to the role of icon, it had been a shock to suddenly find his self consumed by this little boy's ever expanding shadow. How effortlessly Daniel had obscured him; like a lunar eclipse, it was not an event, the world did not darken – and all but he had failed to notice.

Spontaneity did not come naturally to Derek. The sense of pride he enjoyed in his meticulous accounting mirrored his attitude to most things. However, without thinking, he'd plucked the telephone receiver from its cradle and was dialling the number before he'd had chance to consider what he was going to say. The dial tone's uneven drone instilled in Derek a mild panic and when a deep cheerful voice answered "Hello, who's this?" Derek flinched and it took him a few seconds to find his voice.

"Hello."

"Sorry, I can't hear you, bit of a party going on here!"

In the background Derek could hear the sound of laughter, boisterous voices and the implausible pulse of some loud, indistinguishable music.

"Daniel, it's Derek"

There was a pause then a short, embarrassed laugh.

"Brother Derek! My God, how are you?"

"Very well, thank you. Penny and the kids, are they okay?"

"Yes, fine. We're all well. Had a nice break. Took the kids down to mum's in Devon. She's got a lovely little cottage all to herself down there. Have you seen it?"

Derek had neither seen the cottage nor his mother in over a year. It wasn't for any particular reason that they never saw each other. There was no bad blood between them. It was simply that she'd moved out of London after the death of their father and for most of the ten years since, had lived in Brighton, sharing a pretty little flat with her sister near the Marina. Last year, when her sister passed away, Derek's mother decided that the countryside could offer more peace (and opportunity to practice her landscapes) than the noisy arcades and overcrowded coffee houses of Brighton beach.

"I'm an old woman now" she had said to Derek, who had caught the train to Brighton one weekend to help her pack.

"No more hippy backpackers, no more vomit and dog dirt on every inch of pavement – just peace and quiet. That's what I need".

Derek wasn't much good at travelling and his mother had seemed very content on her own once she'd settled.

"I don't need you all down here getting under my feet! You boys have got your own lives – although Derek, I must say, why you didn't marry that Cheryl while you had the chance, I'll never know!"

It irritated Derek greatly that no matter where the conversation started, his mother always drifted on to this topic – and always to Cheryl. It wasn't as though she'd even liked her at the time. "Too much mascara!" she'd exclaimed knowingly, as if that had summed up the girl entirely. She was right in the end, it had.

"That was nearly twenty years ago mother!"

"Exactly! See my point?"

It was useless to argue so he didn't and would let her jabber on, pondering what little thing it was in Daniel's life she used to needle him with. Daniel always seemed to handle her better than he could. The fact that her youngest son had granted her three lovely grandchildren to fuss over appeared to absolve him of all sins, past and present. In spite of his recklessness, Daniel had done well and built a good life for himself and his family – very good it would seem, if the four bedroom house in Romford and the collection of late model cars was anything to go by.

"Well Derek, thoughtful of you to ring. We must catch up more often, it's been nice chatting."

Not exactly chatting, thought Derek, a two-minute exchange. Still, it was good to hear his brother's voice again. Just audible above the noise, Derek heard a woman calling Daniel's name.

"Well old boy, that's my cue. More champagne to be popped!" And he laughed - a rich, satisfied laugh that resonated along the line and through Derek like an electric current.

"Well I won't keep you. Give my best to Penny"

"Oh of course, will do, will do"

"Happy New Year Daniel"

"Oh *haha* God yes, almost forgot. Happy New Year!"

There was a soft click as the music, laughter and voices vanished. Derek carefully returned the receiver to its cradle, picked up his empty glass and went to the kitchen to get more wine.

Hidden

Margaret awoke, grudgingly aware that her flannelette nightie had ridden up whilst she'd slept and was now wrapped tightly around her like an over-sized bandage. She was also painfully aware of the pronged plastic roller pressing against her left temple and after a short wrestle with the offending nightdress, shifted her weight slightly, re-adjusting her curlers in the hope of relief and another ten minutes sleep.

The bedroom door stood open and Margaret lay facing away from it; eyes still closed with the quilt tucked under her chin, listening to Joe's impatient grumble drifting up from the passageway as he stumbled back and forth in the half-light, searching for his coat. Honestly, If only he'd hang it up at night like she asked him, he wouldn't be in such a tizz each morning. She smiled; if it wasn't that, it'd be something else - he liked his little self-righteous flap-abouts, did Joe. In fact, it occurred to Margaret that her husband had always appeared to be at his most content whilst tutting and cursing at something - including her. She'd gotten used to it now and knew he didn't mean anything by it; it was just his way.

Twenty-two years of marriage were worth a few concessions and turning a blind eye to his increasingly gruff demeanour and the occasional fits of temper had certainly not been the hardest. She stared dolefully across at the dressing table where, had life been different, there would have stood numerous gilt framed photographs of children - perhaps even grandchildren by now, smiling proudly back at her. Margaret shook the thought from her head.

She heard the latch on the front door snap shut and listened for the familiar click clack of steel tipped boots as Joe crossed the narrow street. It had been a cold night and the steep cobbled hill down to the foundry would be icy. From the hoarse grunt he had made as he had levered himself off the mattress that morning, Margaret knew Joe's hip was playing up again. She hoped he wouldn't slip.

Warm and comfortable beneath the quilt, Margaret studied the wallpaper - a coarse wood-chip that (if she remembered rightly) had, at first, been a pretty pastel blue that Joe's mother had taken the liberty of choosing whilst he and Margaret had been at Whitby on their honeymoon. It had rained the entire weekend but Margaret had so loved being near the ocean that she was quite happy just to sit quietly by the hotel window staring out at the brightly coloured fishing boats sailing in and out of the harbour. They'd never returned to the town, which was a shame. Margaret told herself that it had probably changed beyond recognition by now anyway and it was best that she savoured the memory of it as it was rather than be disappointed. She felt a small twinge of melancholy and swiftly guided her thoughts back to the wallpaper. Next had come yellow, which they had both thought quite cheerful and so had kept it that colour, varying the shade every few years until the boredom of a bank holiday weekend (combined with a curious browse through Home & Garden at the doctor's surgery) had inspired Margaret to transform it into a more subtle dusty pink. After much persuasion, Joe had added a rose bud border and at the time Margaret had thought it looked very posh with the delicate petals seamed meticulously to form a chain around the room. He'd done a good job, she'd grant him that. Nearly a decade had passed since then however and during the many winters that had followed, damp had seeped through the brick and into the paper. Panel by panel, like the petals in its design, the border's edges had gradually curled until finally each link in the tenuous chain had been broken. Margaret sighed. 'It's sad really' she thought and then a wry smile crept slowly across her lips, 'You, Margaret Donalds, got everything you chose - count yourself lucky and stop moping!'

It was unusual for her to linger in bed of a morning and wanting to capture this rare moment of laziness just a little longer, Margaret buried her face in the pillow and listened for the rattle of Harry's old milk float that would normally be crawling somewhere along the kerb at this time of day. Harry had been delivering milk to these streets for as long as Margaret could remember. Even the two strokes he had suffered had not dampened the old man's enthusiasm for his daily rounds. The second one had been dreadful, affecting his speech and leaving him with a permanent twitch. Everyone had been sure that was the last they'd see of him. Mrs Turnery at number thirty-six had even been to visit him at the hospital, taking with her a lovely bunch of flowers and a card that the whole street had signed. Imagine their surprise when, three weeks later, there he was, sat at the wheel of his float, waving a cheerful hello at everyone who passed him.

"Good old Harry" she chuckled to herself, "that's the spirit".

No sign of him this morning however, only the prattle of the sparrows outside the window, arguing with their chicks. 'Running late, I imagine' she pondered amiably, 'probably popped into Mrs Jackson's' for a bit of breakfast'. The thought of breakfast teased her reluctantly into motion. Swinging her heavy legs out of bed, Margaret tucked her feet into a pair of slippers, struggled with the quilted nylon housecoat she suspected was now a little too tight for her and trudged downstairs to the kitchen.

Leaning heavily on the yellowed porcelain sink, she gazed out of the window and wrinkled her nose at the empty street. When, as newly-weds, she and Joseph had bought this house, Holden Terrace had seemed awash with soot-ingrained husbands, biscuit baking wives and hyperactive children ceaselessly commandeering the pavement with pushbikes and pogo sticks. It had endlessly annoyed Joe to hear their shrill voices echoing from street to street as they played hide and seek, teasing each other from the safety of their hiding spots and squealing indignantly once found. Margaret on the other hand, had loved it; the constant chatter of young voices was to her, like birdsong. Many times at dusk, whilst getting Joe's tea ready, she used to stand at the sink listening to the mothers call out for their young to come indoors. Sometimes she would pretend to do the same. Dropping the potato peeler and wiping her hands on her apron, Margaret would walk to the back door and stand there a moment, with her forehead pressed against the cold wood, clutching the bolt handle. It was a foolish game that often made her cry; but she played it all the same. Margaret, who was normally a very practical woman, really hadn't thought as to why she had been gripped by such a peculiar habit – or perhaps she had but had wisely made the decision not to analyse it. After all it was only a game; just one of the many things Margaret had let slip inside the emotional buffer she'd so carefully constructed over the years.

Eventually the pretence had worn thin and the game had ended. Time passed slowly (although now of course, it seemed to her to have flown by) and from that same window, Margaret had watched the children grow up and disappear one by one, escaping to distant, more modern suburbs with semi-detached houses and high rise flats. Gradually, the friendly little terrace had drifted into a sleepy existence and the life she and Joe shared, pleasant but uneventful. 'Hmm, not completely true' Margaret reconsidered coyly, reaching across the draining board to part the curtains. 'It has its moments'.

She caught a glimpse of her reflection in the glass. "You have beautiful green eyes," Joseph had told her when they 'd first started courting. And it was true, they had been - but just as she had watched his smile tighten to a grimace as age crept sulkily across his face; had he in turn seen her once spirited, sparkling gaze become pallid? Had it upset him to watch her fade? As the thick cotton slid apart, milky sunlight poured into the kitchen and with it the faint clink and muffled 'good mornings' of Harry collecting empties from a nearby doorstep.

"Quite right Harry," exclaimed Margaret as if the thought had escaped her, "Time to start the day."

After folding the last of Joe's shirts into the twin tub, Margaret filled the kettle, dropped two slices of white bread into the toaster and pottered about the kitchen waiting for her egg to boil. The doctor had given her quite a stern lecture regarding her beloved daily habit of egg and soldiers. He'd even given her a handful of leaflets to 'help her become more aware' of her cholesterol intake. Two streets from the surgery, she'd thrown them with great disdain, into a nearby dustbin. "Stuff and nonsense!" she'd snorted. "Never done me any harm – or my mother before me".

Margaret's parents had lasted well into their eighties and Margaret fully intended to do the same - with the unerring philosophy of eating whatever good food took her fancy until she had no teeth left to chew with. Food was one of life's pleasures and Margaret saw no reason to deny herself what few luxuries were available to her. That's not to say that she didn't enjoy a couple of glasses of sherry and the occasional night out, but Joe was not a sociable creature and after a long day on the shop floor with all the boisterous young lads around him, he liked his solitude of an evening. Every Tuesday Margaret would go to bingo with the girls from the rotary club. She did look forward to Tuesdays – in a routine so finely honed that she had become dazed by it, Tuesday nights marked the start and end of each week; they'd become a way of measuring time for her.

After breakfast she washed, dressed and struggled into a pair of orange rubber gloves to clean the fridge. 'I ought to get something for tea' she thought, peering dismally into the empty butter compartment after she'd finished. Tugging at the strings of her apron only to find one of them come off in her hand, she scowled, muttering "This old thing's going in the bin that's for sure!" It didn't however, instead she tucked it into the oven rail where she kept the tea towels and was just about to fetch her coat from the passageway when it occurred to her, "The washing will be crumpled if I leave it. Better to hang it out before I go". Her glance fell upon the old grandfather's clock and she froze for a moment; her gaze dragged back and forth by the swing of its pendulum.

Once belonging to Joe's great uncle and given to them as a wedding present, the clock stood in the passage stoically measuring time amongst the coats and boots, the broken brollies and knick knack that two decades had accumulated. Its hollow tick tock, slow and constant, was the heartbeat of the house. Suddenly her hand flew to her stomach as the unexpected spasm gripped her belly and grief shot through her. All the *could have been's* and *never will be's* hit her at once, a vivid kaleidoscope of splintered regrets and unfulfilled longings exploding like firecrackers around her. She felt so old, so tired. The vast canopy of moving colour blurring her vision made her feel small and vulnerable. The faces of people she knew flew past her. Friends, family, neighbours, even past suitors and children; children she did not recognise, children she'd never seen. Margaret closed her eyes and with a steadying grip on the banister, remained perfectly still for a moment listening to her heartbeat slow until it echoed that of the clock and her breath became one with the pendulum. Only then did she pick up the washing basket and take it into the garden.

The high street was quiet: it was Friday; everyone went to town on Friday. Margaret did occasionally, not that she needed anything from there. The village had a good grocer, butcher's shop and post office. There was even a small supermarket that had opened last spring. Most of their clothes they ordered from the Littlewoods catalogue now. At first Joe had huffed and puffed about such unreasonable extravagances but had said nothing since the first package of woollen socks and Y-fronts had arrived; which he had opened wearing the same delighted expression of a child on its birthday. No, it wasn't for what she would find there that she went. It was the bus journey really, forty-five minutes over the dales, stopping at the many single lane villages along the way. They were so peaceful and pretty; like something you'd find on a postcard and Margaret often wondered if the little Mediterranean villages she'd seen on TV looked the same. She and Joe had never travelled together - although Margaret had wanted to. She'd even brought home brochures occasionally in the hope of changing his mind but Joe had simply turned his nose up at them; he just wasn't the adventurous type. A car of course, was out of the question. "Too many of those blasted things on the road as it is" he would bark whenever she mentioned it. They'd had picnics up on the moors occasionally - a good hour's walk from the village on a hot day. Once Joe had picked a nice spot, Margaret would lay the blanket out for them and sit in silence whilst he read the newspaper, with her knees tucked under her chin, searching the distant hills for some small clue of the world that thrived beyond them. Some days, when Joe was in a good mood or had had a little more stout than usual, they would linger there, sharing each other's warmth beneath a blanket whilst the growing darkness swallowed every feature, leaving only the thin ribbons of light from distant motorways tracing patterns in the air like sparklers.

A young woman strolled past with a child in her arms and smiled cheerfully.
"How are you Mrs Donalds?"
Margaret nodded politely.
"Not too bad" she replied. "Thank you".
There was no one in Hobsons' butchers other than Mrs Hobson herself, who was stood at the front window as she always did, hoping to see someone or something interesting to natter about. Mrs

Hobson loved to call her interest in other people's lives 'natter'. Margaret liked to call it snooping.

"Oh Mrs Donalds" the old lady waved at her in a fluster.

"You'll never guess what!" she exclaimed.

"No" answered Margaret, "I probably won't".

The other woman's face cracked into a wrinkled grin.

"Tom Fanshaw, you know Tom, number forty-eight Marlborough Terrace, two up from your - "

Margaret nodded impatiently "Yes, yes Mrs Hobson, I know".

"Well, he's packed his bags and gone. Left Ivy Fanshaw in a terrible mess, you know, what with all her thyroid trouble."

'Fat!' thought Margaret, stifling a smirk.

"Broke her heart he has, the poor love".

Beckoning her friend closer, Mrs Hobson lowered her voice to a conspirital whisper.

"Off with a younger woman they say - and him pushing seventy!"

"Sixty-five, I think" smiled Margaret placidly. Mrs Hobson pulled back in horror.

"As old as that? ... Anyway, Ivy found two airline tickets in his best suit - two, mind you - and when she confronted him, he just up and left. Majorca they were!"

"Pardon?" frowned Margaret

"Majorca" the old woman hissed, "Two tickets to Majorca!"

"Well I never" said Margaret in mocking disbelief, "Half a pound of bacon and four sausages would be lovely Mrs Hobson, if you could". She couldn't help but smile to herself however. 'Majorca.' she thought, 'Fancy that!'

On the way home she picked up a brown loaf knowing that Joe would want a bit of bread with supper. She also bought a can of sardines, he could have those for his breakfast, she decided, and an extra bottle of milk (gold top of course – not that he could tell the difference once it was opened). Then Margaret spent the rest of the afternoon cleaning the bathroom and ironing the laundry she'd put out that morning.

The last of Joseph's shirts hung neatly out to air in the sitting room, Margaret plonked herself at the kitchen table, tuned the black and white to Knots Landing and settled down with a cup of tea and half a dozen ginger biscuits. She had almost an hour to kill before the potatoes needed peeling.

At four, potatoes peeled and in the pan, Margaret put the sausages under the grill, the vegetables on the stove and went upstairs to pack. She returned to the kitchen ten minutes later, carrying a small overnight bag. Walking over to the grill, she turned the sausages then thought better of it and switched the gas off.

"Joseph would be ever so mad if I let them burn," she said to herself, fondly recalling the time she had overcooked the steaks he'd proudly brought back from the butchers. He had never let her forget it - such fuss and bother, the likes she'd never seen. Joe was particular about his food; liked it 'just right'. The problem was that it had taken Margaret most of their twenty odd years together to figure out what 'just right' was. Joseph kept changing his mind – not that he'd ever admit it. The thought made her sigh. It was the strangest of things to love someone's vices as much as you loved their virtues. And he had many of both – as did she, she had to admit. Margaret knew her tendency for reverie infuriated Joseph who was constantly remonstrating her for not listening to him. In all fairness, it was difficult for her. In recent years, Joseph had taken to mumbling – usually in the form of grumbling monologues and Margaret was often unsure as to whether he was actually talking to her or not. Every once in a while he would interrupt himself and fire a question at her, taking her by surprise so that she would have to ask him to repeat it. The furrow in his brow would deepen and Joseph would mutter words like 'inattentive' and 'irritating', which would then trail into another monologue. At this point he would get up from the table and wander into the sitting room to smoke a woodbine and listen to the news on the radio, content to surrender his soliloquy to that of the faceless newsreader. However, half an hour later, knowing Margaret would have finished the dishes and be looking forward to putting her feet up, he would return, tiptoeing carefully across the kitchen with a delicate sherry glass in each large, rough skinned hand, trying not to spill the sticky syrup wine he had brought as a peace offering.

"Bless you Joseph," she murmured, "you're a good man."

There was a Radio Times on the table and she flipped it over, reached for a pen and wrote on the back of it *Hope you had a good day at work, dinner needs re-heating, take care of yourself Joseph - love Marg.*

Keys still on the dresser, she left the house and walked to the end of the street.

As she passed number fifty-two, Mrs Tanner waved at her from the window. Margaret smiled and tipped her head in return but quickened her pace and kept her gaze towards the pavement. Now was not the time to get caught in conversation.

At the corner stood a pleasant looking gentleman who smiled nervously as she came towards him. He was very slender and his frame, obviously once tall and proud, was now a little stooped. His eyes were cobalt blue and twinkled as he turned to face her.

"Tom Fanshaw" she smiled coyly, "You're wearing your best suit in my honour"

He gripped her hand, regarding her with open admiration.

"You've never seen it before Margaret, how did you know it was my best?"

"Oh" she laughed, "a little bird told me".

Suddenly Tom's face crumpled into an uncertain frown. Fear crept into his voice and he spoke so timidly Margaret could barely hear him.

"Still sure?"

Over Tom's shoulder, Margaret saw winter's pale sun sinking into the moors and thought of the narrow cobbled street that lay behind her. This village represented her entire life. Fifty-eight years ago, Margaret Joyce Davis had been born just four streets from this very spot. She had been christened and then married in the small church that stood less than a mile from here and – had she been content to stay, would have died in her sleep next to her husband and been buried in the same sacred earth on which she took her vows. An entire life spent hidden amongst the moors in this idle Yorkshire village.

"Absolutely" she replied, and placed a hand gently on his cheek.

Tom Fanshaw could not mistake the certainty in her voice and reassured, his weathered face split into a grin. Tall and proud once more, he took her arm in his. "Ready then?"

For the first time in many years, Margaret's face blushed pink with anticipation. 'A brand new life' she thought, 'in a whole new world'.

"Ready as I'll ever be Tom Fanshaw." She laughed, "Ready as I'll ever be!"

Raffle Boy

"That's your third book this week son. Something special going on at school is there?" The newsagent regarded the young boy warily as he handed him his change. Callum took the change and picked up the raffle tickets, thrusting both into the pocket of his shorts. Then, lifting his face to meet the newsagent's gaze, he responded evenly. "Nah, fitba' - we huvnae got an away strip for the finals so coach has organised a raffle."

The old man's frown lifted instantly. Time and drink had erased all trace of it, but as a younger man he'd been a keen footballer. Most lads around these parts were; three decades had changed little. With life in the shipyards an inevitability for all but the brightest and more adventurous, the young men of Glasgow's inner west had always fallen heavily to dreaming of bigger, better things – of glories on the pitch at Ibrox or Hampden, and the mythical stadiums of Europe they knew in their hearts they'd never see.

"Are ye on the team then?"

"Aye," Callum answered. "I'm captain."

The newsagent spread his arms in delight. "Ach, good on ye son! Captain eh?" He reached into the cash register and took out a pound note. "Decided on a colour?"

Tensing, Callum gazed back at him blankly. "Colour?" he said, "Whit d'ye mean?"

"For yer away strip ye daft wee bugger!"

"Ach, yellow, I think."

The old man raised a questioning eyebrow but nodded his acceptance. "What's the prize then?"

Callum realised he was back in safe territory. "Whisky!" he answered brightly. "Mrs Roberts won the last one – bottle o' Glenfiddich."

"Oh aye?" the newsagent nodded, impressed. "I'll take a few myself son – seeing as it's for a good cause, you know." He handed the note to the boy. "Ha many will that get me?"

Callum pulled the raffle book back out of his pocket and ripped out five tickets.

"For ye, that many." he quipped confidently, handing them to the newsagent. "Can I borrow yer pen so's I can write yer name on the stubs?"

The old man tucked the tickets into his shirt pocket and passed Callum the pen he'd been holding. "When exactly is this raffle wee man?"

Callum had his answer ready. "Sunday. I'll let you know what happens. Ye ne'er know, I might be back wi' a bottle!"

The old man chuckled, rubbing his tumescent belly with a sausage-fingered hand. "Aye lad that ye might. Let's hope so shall we?"

Callum had one foot on the pavement when he heard the newsagent's voice urgently calling him back. His heart began to race wildly; another second and he'd have been gone.

"Hey, son!" Callum heard him call again.

"What?" he yelled back, unwilling to move. He'd be damned if he was going back into the shop. If he was about to get collared, Callum knew had had a better chance of escape out on the street, so instead he remained half in, half out, wedging the heavy shop door open with his foot, his palm pressed flat against the glass as a precaution.

"What colour's yer home strip then?"

Callum froze. That was the one thing he hadn't thought of; no-one had ever asked him that before. He realised this could go either way. Built to accommodate both the Faifley and Drumchapel estates, the shopping centre sat beside the playing fields frequented by the elder students from Clyde Bank's two nearby high schools. Catholic and Protestants alike kicked about there, smoking and playing football and it was therefore considered neutral territory. As he'd walked toward the shopping centre from his school, Braidfield High, (a proudly protestant institution according to his maths teacher, Mr Brannan), Callum had often seen lads in Celtic strips and scarves not only outside the shops, stuffing their faces with crisps and chocolate, but in the neighbouring playing field as well. (Callum made a mental note of this for the journey home. The last thing he needed with a pocketful of raffle ticket money was to encounter a gang of 'greens'.) Who was to say the shopkeeper himself wisnae a greenie? Faced with a fifty-fifty chance, Callum went with his instincts. "Uh, blue."

The newsagent nodded sombrely. "Good lad. The way it should be. There's tae many o' those feen'an bastards aroun' here!"

Callum smiled and waved a cheerful goodbye to the old man. It was a warm summer's afternoon, school was over and the weekend was just beginning. Callum wondered whether to head towards Faifley of Drumchapel, his old stomping ground. In a rare moment of indecision, he flipped a coin. Drumchapel it was.

"Hello there, Cal, nice ta see you. How's yer ma?"

Callum had just reached the edge of the estate when saw Terry McGowan's mum coming toward him, carrying a toddler in one arm and pushing an empty stroller with the other. Callum greeted her with a shy nod and stood patiently, watching her berate the child squirming on her hip. His hand tucked inside the pocket of his shorts, fingering the raffle book, he contemplated selling her a ticket then thought better of it. Best to stay away from familiar faces, he decided - you never knew who your ma might run into down at the shopping centre.

Mrs McGowan packed the grumbling child back in its stroller.

"Well, say hello to yer mother for me won't ye?"

Callum shuffled past her. "Aye, aye, I will." He waited until they had turned the corner before scanning the street and deliberating his next move. "Well then," he mused, "Where'll I start?"

As always, Drumchapel was a hive of activity. Around him Callum could hear the drone of human life, not only in the surrounding streets, but also behind every front door. Bar several futile attempts at individuality, such as the odd colour deviation or those large ornate brass numbers favoured only by homeowners and the unnecessarily proud, every one was identical - each garish blue door marking out the territory of Glasgow's rowdiest clans. Row after row of red brick facades; council flats piled on top of each other, their unkempt gardens spewing out clutter onto the wastelands beyond. Decades of poverty and unemployment had loosened the council's grasp on this troubled gathering hole. Caravans in tow, travellers came and went, staking their claim on what green land they could find until the powers that be no longer cared about the mounting garbage, the graffiti, the overcrowding.

Left to its own devices, the estate's boundaries had continued to edge outwards, spreading like a rash towards the city of Glasgow. Callum had walked these streets many times. He'd actually spent most of his life in nearby Faifley, born and bred in one of the two story council blocks that visiting social workers liked to call town houses, but Drumchapel was home to most of his school friends and therefore a second home to him. Young children, some still sporting their uniforms, dotted the pavements, sitting amongst the litter and dog shit, casting marbles against garden walls in fierce competition with each other; or throwing stones at the older kids who whizzed past them on souped-up choppers.

Callum took care not to pick the flat numbers of those who might know him. There'd been no answer at number thirty-four (even though he was sure he'd heard the faint, familiar strains of Crackerjack from beyond the door.) Now he stood, staring at the flat across the landing. That one was no good either, he reasoned. Johnny Pearson lived there and, although not a pal of his, it was common knowledge that Johnny and he were on the same under twelve's team, training together every Thursday night. Next to Callum, Johnny was the team's star player. His father would stand on the sidelines every Sunday, yelling at his son to run faster. "Shift yer fat arse ye lazy wee bastard!" was the standard refrain. It seemed to be the only encouraging statement Johnny's father knew. After each match, the coarse, witless man would repeat the insult, swiping at his young son as he approached him, threatening to clout Johnny if he didn't do better the next week. Callum felt sorry for his teammate. "Better no da at a' than a bully like that." he thought. No, Callum decided, he would leave number thirty-six alone: there was no way Johnny's ma wouldn't know about the away strip raffle – if there was one.

Less than an hour later, Callum was on his way back down Drumry Boulevard towards the cemetery with a book of raffle stubs and a substantial amount of change in his pockets. He was feeling pleased with himself, he had done well. As he passed Saint Columbus' High School, he kept a sharp eye out for brown blazers and banded white and green sweat shirts, recalling his earlier resolution to stay out of trouble. Friday night was traditionally fight night. In his 'enemy' uniform of grey shorts and jumper, Callum was an obvious target.

Added to this the fact that his school shorts jangled ostensibly with a small fortune of silver, today the usually brash young lad felt vaguely vulnerable, in spite of his good mood. He had sold thirty-four tickets, which, including the five that the newsagent had taken earlier, brought Callum's collection to a sum total of six pounds and eighty pence. Gleefully, he thought of the jar of coins beneath his bed: the proceeds of the two books of tickets he'd sold on Wednesday evening and at school the day before. There must be twenty quid in there, he reckoned – or close to it. Callum's chest swelled with the sensation of wealth. "Champion! Champion!" he sang quietly as he swaggered down the main road, relishing the weight of the change in his pockets.

It would have been quicker to walk down Queen Mary Avenue, but it was a nice evening and he was feeling sentimental. As he circled the roundabout, passing the turn-off to Faifley, Callum stopped and gazed along it wistfully, observing the subtle curve of the pavement's edge, like a tramline, disappearing into the distance.

He'd liked living there – despite the trouble his mother had suffered at the hands of their unscrupulous in-laws. Once his dad had gone for good, the rest of his clan had swarmed upon the family home as if it were an abandoned nest. Like greedy scavengers, they'd brushed his mother aside, spitting and swearing as they hauled away what few possessions her husband had left her. Not content with watching his gambling drunkard son steal his young wife's dignity (along with the balance of their joint account), Callum's granddad had quickly laid claims to most of the furniture that had not already been pawned. "Heirlooms" he had called them, dragging them roughly down the stairwell and out into the street. So hurried were they to retrieve what they could that they had forgotten to hire a van to take away their booty and consequently uncle Jim (the eldest brother of three and as much a gambler as Callum's dad) had demolished some of the larger pieces, wrenching the legs off the dining table so that it would fit into the back of his Ford Capri.

"Ach, bit o' glue, they'll be fine," he had reassured Callum and his little sister, Maggie, as they'd stood open mouthed with confusion and horror.

Their brother, James, who was three years older than Callum (and named in his uncle's honour) had snorted derisively in response and mumbled "Fucking philistine" just loud enough to be heard. It had earned him a well-placed slap across the head from his uncle and James had staggered backwards and fell against the hedge – the overweight, red-faced man watching his namesake stumble with great amusement. Their grandfather, who had seen the exchange from the passenger seat of his son's car, leant across the driver's side and called impatiently to him through the open window.

"Get in the car Jim. We'll get nothing for our trouble if we're not a' Michael's ba four."

Callum knew then that the jumble of wood poking out of the boot, and the bronze, china and silverware on the back seat of his uncle's dirty yellow Capri were not heirlooms. Michael was the name of the local moneylender who ran a second hand shop out of a garage on the Drumchapel Estate – everyone knew Michael. Suddenly it had dawned on Callum; his granddad and uncle had raided their small house for valuables, even taking the furniture with the sole intention of pawning it. Callum turned in search of his mother to see her expressionless face at the kitchen window. Why hadn't she come out, he wondered. Why hadn't she done something? The three children had looked on helplessly as the car pulled away. The rest of the day, Callum had ignored his mother, answering her only when necessary in a sullen, resentful tone. It was only after he'd gone to bed that night and heard her crying in the half empty sitting room that he fully understood: there had been nothing she could do. The strong, fearless woman he'd imagined his mother to be, who everyday, went out to work before dawn, washed their clothes and cooked their meals was, Callum realised with a sinking heart, as helpless as her children.

By the time he had reached the cemetery, it was almost dark. Feeling too conspicuous on the main path, Callum began to edge his way gingerly between the gravestones. By day, the graveyard was a common shortcut between Callum's high school and the shopping centre and it was not unusual to pass half a dozen other people heading to and from school or the ring road beyond. By night, however, the graveyard's tranquil beauty distorted into something far more menacing. A refuge for tramps needing a quiet corner out of the wind, in the half-light the headstones seemed to loom towards him, harbouring the silent threat of someone or something lurking behind. In truth, it was not the threat of the old drunks that made the soft hair on his arms stand proud despite the warm evening air, but the thrill of what dangers Callum's imagination could conjure into existence. The drunks were usually harmless, retired ship workers who, in their stupor, often roamed into the cemetery so that they might nestle against one of the weathered slabs and sleep off the effects of their long day in the pub. Most had wives and homes to go to once they'd sobered up, but some had neither and it was of these poor souls that Callum was most wary. He could not understand why a man would spend his life hovering, albeit unwittingly, between dispensaries of drink and death. It reminded Callum of a film he'd watched on television one rainy Sunday afternoon; a black and white film about a miserable old man called Scrooge who seemed to Callum as close to death as any living being could be. He'd understood that the story had been about miserliness and greed, but it was the emptiness of the man's life that had struck Callum – and the isolation of solitary existence. Why would any man want that, he wondered. To have lost your family through death or divorce, grown old and abandoned by your selfish children, these were the vagaries that life threw at you – but to willingly, defiantly amputate yourself from your kin, your children, why would any man choose to do that? Callum knew that somewhere, perhaps nearby, perhaps on the east side of Glasgow, was his da. Family friends had often approached his ma with tales of her husband's whereabouts. He'd been spotted in a lot of places in the three years since he'd left; mostly amidst the smoke-filled bars and betting shops that dotted Clyde Bank - and once on a street corner, propping up his swaying frame against a traffic sign.

For some reason Callum always pictured him sitting in a cafe, supping from a sturdy mug of tea. His da like his tea strong - strong enough so that the tannin formed scum patches on the viscous orange surface, with two heaped sugars 'to take the edge off'. Callum had always wondered what his da had meant by that. He'd never drunk tea – or coffee for that matter, it seemed senseless to take up the less palatable drinking habits of adulthood when there was so much else on offer. Callum, a connoisseur of Irn Bru and chocolate milk, associated the hot, bitter tasting drinks with the brooding silence of his father and the intimate forums of his mother and her friends around the kitchen table; sombre adult worlds in which he had no part.

Callum's thoughts drifted back to his da. Sometimes he imagined him not in a bright bustling café but sorrowful and alone, like the old man in the film – or with a pint slopping over one hand, a cigarette in the other, slurring and deluded, being thrown out of a pub. But, for reasons he did not understand, what appeared to Callum mostly was the image of a tidy tenement flat, his father's sturdy frame slumped contentedly on the settee, and a woman beside him, the TV's glare reflected in their complacent faces. The woman's face was always clearer, a composite of imagined features, whereas, due to the disappearance of family photos (along with the worthless wooden frames his grandpa and uncle had taken to pawn three years previously) Callum's memory of his father's face had diminished and now he saw only shadows about the man, a faceless image like the eye witnesses they interviewed on TV documentaries. Was it a better life his da was living now? Had he found the type of family he'd always wanted, Callum wondered. When his da had first left them, confused and betrayed by his mother's silence on the subject, Callum had assumed that it had been some failing of their own unruly clan that his da had turned away from – and that out there, somewhere, was the type of family he really wanted: a good wife and clever, respectful children that did as they were told. Once, in a moment of weakness, he'd confided this to Jimmy who had laughed scornfully in response and told him to 'get lost'. Now that he was older and knew better, Callum sneered at his own naiveté. Jimmy was right. Why would his da bother with another man's kids when he could simply find himself a new wife and make more of his own? Perhaps there were others out there, mused Callum; another little sister like Maggie, or a baby brother for him to tease, just as Jimmy teased him.

"That's just stupid." Callum reasoned aloud, kicking away a loose clump of earth from a nearby gravestone. "After a' it's no' like they'd be family or anything."

Safely through the graveyard now and less than ten minutes from home, Callum relaxed his grip on the silver in his pocket, letting it jangle freely against his thigh as he strode. As he reached the outskirts of Old Kilpatrick, it occurred to him that he'd not visited Mrs Mackintosh yet that week and that she'd be wondering where he was. Mrs M, as Callum liked to call her, was a friendly old lady who lived on the outskirts of Old Kilpatrick. Callum had known her all his life; she had lived next door to them back in Faifley and had taken a keen interest in their welfare after his da had left. (Callum had had it drummed into him by his mother more times than he could remember not to forget the old woman's kindness.) Eventually her arthritis had gotten so bad she could no longer climb the stairs to her bedroom and had taken to sleeping in her favourite armchair with a blanket over her knees. Her eldest son, a bank manager who now lived in Stirling, had taken pity and bought her a bungalow bordering one of the many newly built estates that had unrepentantly devoured most of the barren land flanking the shores of the Clyde. It was on a nice street, with flowers of every colour spilling out of small, tidy gardens. The bungalow was cute (in a biscuit tin kind of way) with whitewashed walls and royal blue window frames, their glossy hue painted to match both the garden gate and the front door. Callum liked to visit there, and Mrs Mackintosh always had a chocolate bar or packet of crisps to give him for his trouble. One of Mrs M's weaknesses was her fondness for pop. "I cannae help it Callum," she'd crow whenever he saw her. "I know all those bubbles are bad for a gassy ol' thing like me – and ach, all that sugar! But still…" she'd pause and drain the last of the Irn Bru from her glass. "Life's too short an' so ye cannae say no tae a little bit o' heaven now an' then!"

Gassy or not, Callum certainly wasn't going to discourage her. Each week, the old woman's sweet tooth powered her through, on average, two tall bottles of Irn Bru, one of Cream Soda and an extensive assortment of fruit flavoured fizzy pop. At ten pence return on each bottle, a visit to Mrs M's was usually good for at least fifty – sometimes a quid when her grandchildren had stayed over for the weekend.

Mrs Mackintosh was in her front garden, clasping a trowel in one gloved hand and a clump of weeds in the other. As Callum approached the bungalow, she waved; the weeds shuddered, raining seeds and loose soil that she then shook awkwardly from her hair, making the lose knot on the top of her head wobble somewhat comically. Callum smiled at her with genuine affection as he returned her wave.

"Hi there Mrs M. Sorry I huvnae been by – hard week at school."

"Ach ye poor wee thing. Too much homework eh?"

Grinning broadly, the fat, pleasant-faced old woman tucked the small trowel into the pocket of her tunic, throwing the weeds into a large yellow bucket at her feet.

"A couple of chocolate biscuits might just perk ye up!" Gesturing him to follow her, she stepped back onto the garden path and made her way cautiously towards the front door. Callum could see that she was hobbling a little.

"Are yer knees hurtin' ye again?" he asked, already knowing her answer.

"Aye they are, they are. A' should nay complain though. At least they're ma own." She glanced back over her shoulder and winked. "A' cannae say that fer ma teeth!"

Callum smiled. He had often overheard his ma and Mrs M talking about the state of her knees and the insidious arthritis that had gradually begun to consume her. His ma had nagged at Mrs M to apply for a set of new ones. "Ach Esme, they can replace all sorts nowadays. Hips, knees – I know of one fella got a metal plate in his head!" Supping their tea, the two women would ooh and aah at the wonders of technology, but invariably the pensioner would end the conversation with a resigned shake of her head and let it drop low as if suddenly it were much too heavy. "Ach Louise, a'm an old thing now. A' know a' have danced ma last Kaylee."

At this point, the young mother would glance across at her son and smile sadly, signifying it was time to go.

Callum studied Mrs M's gait as they ambled along the hallway to her kitchen. It was a fascinating concept to Callum that a person could be made bionic. The thought of steel- hinged joints and metal plates brought to mind images of the six million dollar man sprinting across sun scorched plains with that strange, electronic sound effect that made Callum think of springs and girders.

"Don't worry about the biscuits Mrs M, I ca' nay stay, a've missed me tea and ma'll be worried."

Esme Mackintosh regarded the young boy with a wry smile.

"Aye, you'll no want te miss the ice-cream van a'll bet."

Feeling acutely transparent beneath the old woman's gaze, Callum studied the scuffed tips of his school shoes. They'd seen better days, he decided. With a chuckle, Mrs M lifted a doughy arm and gestured towards the far end of the kitchen where half a dozen empty pop bottles stood in two neat rows beside the back door.

"I'll get a carrier bag." Esme mumbled as she bent awkwardly to retrieve one from the cupboard under the sink. Callum took it from her and shook it out to check its size.

"Is it big enough?"

"Aye, aye, grand – thanks."

"Will ye tell yer ma a've that sewing pattern fer her?"

"Aye, I will." He hesitated. "Uh, d'ye want me tae take it tae her?"

Again, Esme smiled at him, her pale blue eyes full of warmth and wisdom.

"A young man doesnae need ta be meeting his friends on the street with silly women's things tucked under his arm."

At that moment Callum loved Mrs M. She was as magical and mysterious to him now as she had been when he had stared at her with the eyes of a three year old, wondering whether the wizened old face was that of a witch or a fairy Godmother. The bottles were heavy. Callum shifted the bag from one hand to the other.

"I'd better go."

"Aye, ye had. It's almost half past seven." The old woman shuffled him into the hallway.

"What time does the van come?"

"Eight." Callum answered. "I won't forget to tell ma – ye know, 'bout the pattern."

"Yer a good lad" Esme Mackintosh looked on fondly as Callum, the wee bairn she had once held in her arms, opened her front door and stepped out into the evening.

There was little left of the light by the time Callum had trudged his way through the estate towards his own house – only a marbled peach and crimson glow seeping out of the horizon. Callum's house was bigger than Mrs M's and much bigger than the house they'd had in Faifley. Callum had liked living in Faifley, but he liked having his own room much more. He'd dedicated the wall above his head to Rangers' posters, his favourite being the centrepiece: Davie Cooper, mid stride with the ball at his toe, riding the air like Achilles. (Jimmy had told him that; Jimmy liked that kind of stuff – history and everything. He'd explained to Callum that Achilles was a god and that long ago the Greeks, like the Indians, had not just one god, but lots of them.) Davie cooper was Callum's god – or his hero at least. One day Callum intended to dodge and tackle his way across the pitch at Ibrox, just like Davie.

"Cal, where on earth have ye been?"

Dumping the bag of bottles on the empty tray of his go-cart, Callum turned to see his mother leaning out of the bedroom window, with her arm outstretched, her hand gripping the old fashioned handle-latch.

"Mrs M's ma!" he called out, pointing vaguely over his shoulder. "Picked up her bottles!"

"Ye missed yer tea. Did'na no tell ye to come straight home from school?"

"Aye, aye, sorry. Can a' just take these to Pazza? A' wilnae be a minute – then a'll be in!"

As if on cue, the clunking chimes of Pazza's van punctured the air, declaring its presence in the street beyond. Callum held his mother's stare, widening his grin into a zipper-like grimace, silently pleading his release.

"Ach go on then. But don't think a'll be cooking yer something now – no' at this time o' night! You'll make do wi' a sandwich."

With that her arm folded, bringing the window with it. Callum took up the cart's steering rope and began to manoeuvre it down the path and through the gate. He could hear the clumsy refrain of Greensleeves in the distance. No doubt once he'd turned the corner, Pazza would see Callum and pull the ice-cream van up somewhere nearby. Callum dragged the cart behind him to the lay-by, knowing it was the safest place for Pazza to stop. As he'd predicted, seconds later the van appeared. It wasn't your usual type of ice-cream van, often impregnable except for the serving hatch. Pazza's van had a doorway framing two steep metal steps that you climbed up to enter. Once inside you were free to browse amongst the displayed selection of sweets, crisps, pop and ice creams. Not only did Pazza sell you things, he bought from you as well. Realising there was money to be made from recycling the tall clear bottles that stood forgotten beside the bins in most of his neighbour's back gardens, Callum had quickly begun collecting them and selling them on to Pazza. (It amazed him that folk would be so lazy as to throw things of value into the dustbin just to save themselves a two-minute walk.) There were a couple of other lads on the estate who did the same, but none of them applied themselves to it quite so industriously as Callum. Every Friday Callum would trail his loaded cart out onto the pavement and wait for Pazza to arrive. And every Friday, without fail, at eight o'clock (or thereabouts) the old white van would appear at the corner, pull to a stop beside Callum and Pazza would step down and take the bottles from him, counting out their value at ten pence apiece. Their weekly rendezvous had gradually inspired a rapport between the two. Pazza quietly admired the young boy's initiative; having arrived in Scotland from Italy seventeen years previously with nothing in his pockets but the address of a boarding house on the outskirts of Glasgow and two sterling pound notes, Pazza liked to think of himself as an entrepreneur and saw it as his duty to encourage the lad to build his own empire, just as he had done. Still in possession of an untamed imagination, with an unwritten future ahead of him, Callum didn't think Pazza's mobile snack bar much of an empire - but he appreciated the older man's interest in him and never voiced his condescension.

"What have you got for me today then Cal?" Pazza called out as he climbed from the driver's seat into the back of the van. He stood on the top step, his hairy olive skinned forearms pressed against the doorframe, waiting for Callum to draw the loaded cart closer and then reached down and deftly scooped up both bags of bottles.

"How many is there here then?"

"Fourteen I think. You'd better count 'em, I'm no sure."

Pazza peered into one bag, then the other. "Spot on Cal. Fourteen it is." He laughed, tickled by Callum's coyness. The lad always knew exactly how many bottles there were, but had a curious habit of testing Pazza. This had become a ritual for them. What had once annoyed the humble, honest Italian, piquing memories of his youth as an immigrant feeling alienated by distrust, now gave him a quiet delight as he recognised Callum's wariness as nothing more insidious than a mark of the lad's own stealthy character. Their tacit understanding only added to the very pleasant sense of belonging that Pazza now enjoyed. When the local children clamoured on to his van, jabbering with their friends excitedly about the treats in store for them, he felt a surge of fatherly tenderness. Between them and himself he saw no boundaries other than that of generation. His once thick singsong accent now softening to an unusual brogue, when he served them Pazza saw no reflection in their eyes of an unwelcome foreigner, no retaliation for the subtle differences that still set him apart. Modest as Pazza's empire was, its true value to him was the acceptance into a community whose perception of him was as a figure of trust and munificence. He understood that there was very little power in it – or glory, but non-the less it had brought him great peace. As Callum counted the change Pazza had poured into his hand, the tubby middle-aged man looked on benevolently.

"All there Cal?"

"Aye." Cal smiled in response. "All there. See yer next week yeah?"

"That you will." With that mumbled response, Pazza climbed back into the driver's seat and started up the engine. Callum watched the van stutter back to life and trundle away, turning at the next corner. Callum liked Pazza - Pazza was nice. And Callum was one pound-forty richer.

"I said one minute Callum!" His mother's voice accosted him from the sitting room as he closed the front door and kicked off his shoes.

"And don't go kicking off those muddy school shoes. You're making marks on the wallpaper!"

Callum stared guiltily at the new dark skid mark one of his boots had just created and tried unsuccessfully to erase it with a cotton socked toe. "Nae bother ma!"

He could hear the noise of the television. Football was on – that meant Jimmy was home. Jimmy was starting to stay out at the weekends and come home late most weeknights. It was unusual for him to be lounging around on a Friday night. More often he was out playing football with his mates or getting ready to head into town.

Although only fifteen, Jimmy, like most lads, had already begun the pilgrimage to Glasgow's city centre on the weekends, drinking in whatever bars would serve them and then, emboldened by ale and cheap whisky, scouring the late night streets, their heads swimming with the prospect of girls or warfare – whichever crossed their paths first. That's not to say Jimmy was a fighter. No, Jimmy was a thinker, trailing behind the others when conflict arose, quietly calculating his subtle escape and safe passage home whilst his drunken comrades scuffled with their prey.

When their da had first left, Jimmy had been like a shadow at their mother's side, watching her quietly, unquestioningly – as if ready to catch her should she at any minute fall into a faint. It had seemed to Callum then, who was angry at his ma for his da's disappearance – certain that she lay at the heart of his da's rejection of them, that Jimmy's ghosting of his mother was a sign of weakness, his response to the fear that permeated every room, every smile of his mother's, and clung to their clothes the way the smoke from their da's cigarettes had once done. Now, years on and with what he perceived to be his brother's manhood on the horizon, Callum felt he understood Jimmy better and had begun to miss his elder brother's presence in the house, not relishing the prospect of losing his own carefree middle child status. Instinctively Callum knew that, upon Jimmy's departure, his mother and sister would look to him for protection. He did not want to disappoint them – and had no intention of doing so, but the prospect of a life on the damp and chilly shipyards, coughing up the tar paint that lent its gleam to the underbelly of the monstrous liners or dodging the sparks of a welding torch whilst his hands grew withered and knarled with the wind, was not the future Callum saw for himself. Barely twelve years old, but with a lifetimes' worth of fear and fire already within him, Callum had figured out that in order to avoid the meagre path that so many of Glasgow's young men had trodden before him, he was going to have to become even more inventive.

"You've had ma biscuits, have ye no? There was o'er half a packet left last night!" His gaze still fixed on the screen, Jimmy pointed an accusatory finger at Callum as he swung open the glass door to the sitting room.
"A huvnae!" Callum barked, hoping he'd remembered to plank the empty packet somewhere more cunning than the kitchen bin. He'd been in a hurry that morning, eager to sell his tickets, and without thinking had polished off the six remaining coconut rings that had been sat on the top shelf of the cupboard in an inviting blue wrapper, twisted at one end like an abandoned cracker.
"Ach, don't lie, Ma husnae had them so I know it was you."

"How no?"

"She dusnae like them, and Maggie cannae reach that high!"

Callum knew his brother had him pegged and skulked into the kitchen, hoping Jimmy would remain too engrossed in the game to berate him further. Sometimes Jimmy was like an old woman, Callum mused. On the nights his pals came round to sit with him in his room, nodding their heads knowingly through numerous rock albums, Jimmy would appear from school with a loaded carrier bag, having stopped on his way home at the local supermarket to buy crisps, biscuits and Irn Bru. Ma would laugh and call him 'my little host' and praised her son's thoughtfulness. "You're a good lad." She would often pause and announce tenderly whilst flapping around the house, "Kind – that's we ye are." A mug of tea always in her hand, cooking dinner or getting ready for work, his ma never seemed to stop; like a washing machine Callum decided: stuck on spin cycle whilst all those around her lolled on soak.

There was a large pot on the stove and Callum could smell the faint but familiar aroma of his ma's vegetable soup. He grinned gratefully, proffering his mother a silent thank you and experiencing a tremor of glee at the thought of tasting the tangy tomato based broth. He switched on the stove and buttered a slice of bread. Ma had bought his favourite: Warburton's. Callum loved the way the loaf's greaseproof paper and tanned crust gave way to plump, square white pillows, which, more often than not, he converted into elaborate sandwich extravaganzas and devoured between long sweet gulps of Irn Bru whilst watching the telly.

Beside the kettle, on the Formica top opposite, his ma's handbag sat open – the clasp's thin steel frame agape like the jaws of a gasping fish; her lipstick and compact having tumbled out, lay on the counter beside it. Callum noted the flash of red leather tucked inside the bag's side pocket: his ma's purse. Suddenly Callum remembered the weight of coins in his pocket. How much did he have again? He calculated quickly. Six pounds eighty, actually it was eight – twenty including the bottle money. Not bad, he thought, but not quite a tenner though; it seemed a shame. Listening out for the sounds of movement in the other room but hearing only the drone of the TV, Callum reached inside the bag.

His ma came into the kitchen just as Callum was pouring his soup into a bowl.

"Ach, I see ye found yer dinner then." She scowled good-naturedly and tickled him under the chin. "A'm away tae work now so no fighting you an' Jimmy d'ye hear me? And make sure Maggie gets to bed at a decent hour." Picking up her lipstick and compact, Louise McAllister flipped open the lid on the slim circular case and applied a thick layer of colour to her lips. Smacking them together she first pouted then drew them back into a sneer. Callum observed her curiously.

"Can ye drop us off at the pictures tomorrow Ma?"

"Who's us?" she replied, still examining her face in the compact's small mirror.

"Paul's coming. I'm meeting 'm there."

"What's showing?"

"Dunno."

"Ach, as long as it keeps ye out o' trouble for the afternoon. I've got tae get some shopping and then visit Aunty Mae. You'll be fine catching the bus home will ye no?" She flashed her son a wide smile. "How do I look?"

Callum shrugged and tucked into his soup.

"My, aren't you a charmer?" She laughed and pulled her purse out of her handbag. "You'll be needing some money for tomorrow will ye no? How much are the matinee tickets again?"

Callum bristled. "Ach no ma, I have the bottle money – it's plenty."

His ma continued to peer into the folds of her purse, her brow furrowed in confusion. "That's strange. I don't recall collecting all this change. There must be a tenner's worth of silver in here!"

Tucking the purse back into her bag and slinging it over her shoulder, Louise McAlister reached out to straighten her middle child's soft brown hair. As wild as he was, he was her pride and joy and everything she did, she did for him and Jimmy and Maggie. She bent over and planted a loud kiss on the crown of his head. His hair smelled of summer.

"And here's me worrying what I was goin' tae buy the shopping with. Must have an angel lookin' o'er us eh sweetheart?"

Callum smiled and concentrated on sucking the last of the broth from his spoon.

A Day Out

Mum was just adding the finishing touches to her make-up as I emerged from my bedroom.
"You look lovely darling."
I looked like a mini version of her. My hair was swept away from my face, tied with a silk lilac ribbon, and I had squeezed myself into a short yellow skirt and matching sleeveless top. Twenty horrifying minutes spent deconstructing my body parts in the mirror whilst putting on my make-up had left me feeling both vulnerably underdressed and preened to the point of unnatural.
"You don't think it's a bit much, do you mum?"
"Why? I'm wearing the same!"
That was my point; stretched across her ample bust was a pastel pink version of the very same top I wore and an almost identical skirt that stopped just short of her knees. Suddenly I felt about as sophisticated as a Liquorice All-sort. I envisaged the waiting room, stuffed with stiff lipped women and their sassy starlet daughters; rows of well-tweezed eyebrows raised in a Mexican wave as we passed.
"Listen, maybe I should go change."
Mum scowled. "Don't be silly! Anyway, we're going to be late."
"No we won't, we've got hours."
A furtive smile brightened her face and I knew there was something she hadn't told me.
"Okay mum, what is it?"
The smile spread and broke into a grin. "I've got a date!"
"That's great mum, but what's that got to do with – oh!"
As my heart hit the floor, my face must have followed. All I could say was "This isn't happening".
Mum folded her smile into a clownish grimace, exaggerated and insincere. She was mocking me, hoping I might laugh. "Sweetheart, don't be like that! We're just going to have a quick lunch with Neil and then go straight to the agency, I promise."

She could see I wasn't appeased and distracted herself by rifling through her handbag, pretending to search for her lipstick whilst I stood numbly beside her, unable to speak. I wanted to tell her how important this was; how Philippa - ugly, talentless Pip, who couldn't act her way out of a paper bag and had buck teeth and bad skin, had got herself an acting agent - and how she'd bragged and sneered when I'd said I intended to do the same.

"There's no guarantee of getting one y'know," the pimply creature had drawled in her thick Aussie accent. "Only the really talented ones get picked."

Appalled at the thought that Pip should consider herself more talented than I was, the very next day I sought out the names and numbers of nearly a dozen agents and called each one, asking in a shaky voice if I could come see them. Most were cold and disinterested, others snooty and rude, telling me in supercilious tones that they 'only acquired young talent from reputable stage schools'. In the end, only one was willing to see me, and ironically it turned out be the very same into which my enemy Pip had been accepted. I was joyous.

The receptionist had said that I would need to be accompanied by a parent or guardian. That was okay - I hadn't relished the thought of facing her alone. Mum was delighted when I told her, she didn't even mind that I had to miss school.

"You clever little thing! How exciting – we'll make it a proper day out!"

It had sounded like a great idea. "Something to look forward to" she had said.

Now, stood in front of my mother on the morning of the big day itself, not feeling clever, not feeling excited - and certainly not feeling bright and cheerful, all I could muster was "Who's Neil?"

My mother, who was applying mascara at the time, held the brush against her lashes, pressing in the curl. Only her eyes shifted.

"That's a silly question, Louise!"

"Not really mum – you've never mentioned him before".

"Oh? Haven't I?" She was genuinely surprised. It hadn't occurred to her that I might not know. In her mind I knew everything about her. "Neil is a lovely man that I met the other evening."

"When you went out with Maureen."

"Yes."

"Into town?"
"Yes."
"To the casino."
"Yes."

Conversations were often like this. Years spent being interrogated by my stepfather had honed my mother's skills of tacit response. Although the marriage had faded, the habit had not.

I tried again. "And now we're going on a date with him."
"No."
"No?"
"I'm going on a date with him – you just happen to be there."
"Mum!" It was less of a word and more of a wail.

She threw me one of her 'you're so silly' smiles, "Calm down darling, you'll ruin your make-up. I said we'd meet him at Circular Quay and have some lunch in one of those restaurants on the esplanade. We won't be more than an hour, I promise!"

"Fine!" I spat, stomping into the hall to get my coat. It was obviously a done deal so there was nothing I could do about it. I wanted to make my annoyance felt anyway.

"So, how old am I this time? Nine?"

She cast me a withering glance that died almost instantly, "Err, twelve."

"Mum!"

"Oh sweetie, I'm sorry, it's just that, well, he's very handsome and I think he's a little younger than me…"

"I'm fourteen years old!" I fumed, "Not only that, I'm five foot six and built like a brick shit house!"

"Well, try and look small – and don't swear!" she laughed, flicking the air with her shawl in one swift, graceful move. Almost transparent in the light, the pale silk billowed like a parachute for a moment then fell obediently about her shoulders where she tied it in a knot across her chest. She looked beautiful with the sun streaming in behind her, catching the gold in her hair – like something out of a fabric softener commercial.

"Ready then?" And with that, she was by the front door, flapping her hands like a circus seal.

"Okay, okay, I'm coming!" I growled, grabbing my purse.

"No hurry sweetheart – just drying my nails"

As I passed her she snarled and jabbed my arm, smudging a shell pink nail on my jacket, "And don't even think about wearing that! It's ancient for God's sake!"

"Aw, mum, mow look what you've done." I snapped back, removing the offending article, "It'll take ages to get that off!"

"What I've done?" she cried incredulously, "Look at my nail!" But her face betrayed her with a smug, satisfied smile; she had won the dispute, swiftly and with ease.

The harbour looked stunning. The ferry cut its way through what resembled a deep pool of sapphires; each ripple shimmering like a facet, reflecting the sun. We stood outside, near the helm, so that mum could smoke a cigarette.

"Are you nervous?" she asked me.

"I don't think so. I don't really know what to expect."

That was a lie – or at least the first part; I was in fact, very nervous. I had never been to an interview of such importance before. There had been loads when we had immigrated, doctors and solicitors, bored public servants and kindly school principals, all summarizing and sympathizing. I had sailed through them all uncaring - numbed by the experience of leaving one life for another. This was different. For the first time, I was aware of having to impress my potential upon someone. Now that I had finally been asked to prove its existence, could I? How exactly, would I impress the owner of that crisp, affected voice that had spoken to me over the phone? (I suddenly wondered if the interview would actually be with the woman who'd made the appointment. Perhaps she was just the assistant; perhaps it would be a man, round and jovial with a lecherous grin.) Could I sit in that office, next to my mother of all creatures, being appraised by a stranger – and claim to be special? Some days I felt so, walking home from school so excited by the curiosity of what the future had to offer me that I would have to burst into a skip to avoid imminent explosion.

But then there were the other days. I never knew when they were coming and I had no name for what it was that overpowered me the moment my eyes opened on those mornings, so full of Australian sun and yet greyer to me than any wintry Yorkshire dawn. It was just a feeling, that's all. The air I breathed would be heavy, as if lead were being poured through me, setting in my lungs and threading it's way down my arteries to the tips of my fingers and sometimes my toes. Within seconds sadness would follow, an army of negative thoughts swarming through me like irate bees. Some I would swat away, those I could not would buzz about my head, stinging me throughout the day. With each barb my loneliness became more and more a brooding martyrdom, the belief that it was my karmic duty to bear the brunt of some awful soul who had lived before me. I don't know where exactly the notion came from but it fitted my need to feel sorry for something – and not know what it was.

We were about half way between Manly and Circular quay. Mum's gaze was fixed upon the Opera House, its curved, white peaks framed strangely by the blue and silver towers of the city just beyond it.
"Are you?" I asked
"Am I what?"
"Nervous about your date with Neil?"
Mum cocked her head in the way she always did when she intended to say something matter-of-fact.
"We've chatted on the phone a few times and he seems very nice, very gentlemanly."
I knew that mum wasn't referring to his code of etiquette. She often used words in their most literal sense, and meant that she thought him to be both manly and gentle. That was a good sign. It was a word weighted with expectation, a word said in hope more often than in certainty. 'Gentle-manly' was the marker that one day, one lucky man would finally reach and win my mother's heart.
"I'm glad you're not nervous. So, where are we eating? I'm hungry."
She pulled the pink-rimmed sunglasses she was wearing down on to the bridge of her nose, "Please don't eat too much Louise, you'll be uncomfortable later."
It was meant kindly - as a warning, not a criticism - but instinctively I took it as such and scowled. Mum, knowing very well the effect such statements had on me, deftly changed the subject.
"So this Philippa girl you were talking about, how did she get in to this agency?"

She'd chosen the wrong subject. I felt myself begin to tense with what I thought at the time was annoyance. In fact it was jealousy. Philippa had exactly what I wanted, what I'd dreamed of – a whisper of opportunity, the promise of a phone call that could open doors to a new life. I wanted a new life, a better one than the life that had been chosen for me; it didn't fit and I didn't like it. I changed the subject again.

"Look, we're nearly there! All those people waiting to get on, it must be going straight back."

We were just pulling in, the helm coming level with the head of the pier, and from there I could see the waiting passengers who stood, staring vacantly through the mesh of the gate. Others paced in a restless fashion, tugging at their shirt collars and checking their watches. I studied the lower dock, where we'd be disembarking. I couldn't see anyone and wondered if Neil was the kiss, flowers and handshake type (obviously mum got the kiss and the flowers, the handshakes they reserved for me).

"What does he look like mum?"

"Oh you won't see him there. He's going to meet us on the promenade. Didn't I tell you that?"

"Probably – my mind's drifting".

Mum reached forward and tucked an errant lock of hair behind my ear. "If he's really boring you have permission to spill wine over his shirt and then we can make a dash for it whilst he's in the men's room!"

"Oh, I wish!"

Mum's lascivious humour had finally melted my anger; we both threw our heads back and laughed. I loved my mother's witticisms, and cherished those moments when her wicked streak peeked out from behind that carefully cultivated demeanour.

"The place is on Pitt Street, but I don't know which end."

"Don't worry darling," she said, walking ahead of me to the gangplank, "We'll leave time."

Neil turned out to be very average looking. He was tall, with grey hair and smartly dressed, but too stiff upper lipped to be charismatic. I wasn't impressed and decided instantly that mum was too good for him. It was a beautiful day, full of light, but he insisted on taking us to a steak house in the basement of a nearby hotel.

Descending from the bright street, we took the staircase slowly, adjusting our eyes to the dimness of the restaurant. With dark, thickly varnished wood lining each booth, and once plush, velvet padding on the benches, it was exactly as you'd imagine a traditional steak house to be. I remember clearly, the odour of onions that hung in the air throughout lunch. It was not quite pungent enough to mask the more unpleasant medley of smells that lingered there, the worst of which were cigarette smoke and beef fat. I wasn't expecting to have a good time.

"They have a children's menu, if you want to see one, Louise."

"Why? Is there something funny on it?"

I watched his amiable grin fade and paused for just a second too long, having planned on flashing my placatory 'precocious but sweet' smile at him. Mum got there first. "Louise has a very sharp sense of humour."

I caught the pleading look in her eye and understood that it was not a rebuke. "Sorry, just making a joke."

At the word 'joke' Neil nodded his head sagely, seemingly much relieved by this admission.

"No, no, I got it, very funny. She's bright isn't she?" he said, first looking at me and then my mother in quick succession.

"She is!" we responded simultaneously. His gaze bobbed between us both, unsure of where to rest.

Lunch passed quietly, garnished with forced smiles and pithy statements. Coached by mum not to cause offence by repeatedly asking the time, I searched the walls for a clock. Finally, on the last of my several journeys to the toilet, I peered through the square glass panel of the door that led to the kitchens. There was only a corridor. I was going to have to ask Neil after all. It was getting late, I was sure of it. Just at that moment, a door at the other end of the corridor swung open and a young girl hurried out, carrying what appeared to be a stack of dirty plates. As the door swung closed behind her, I glimpsed the sterile face of a large wall clock. It was already a quarter to three. We'd all been boring each other stiff for two hours. How on earth could the time have passed so quickly, I wondered, striding as calmly as I could, back to the table. Neil had gone to pay the bill.

"Mum, for God's sake it's nearly three o'clock. We've got to go now!" I growled, grabbing her shawl.

"We will soon," she whispered hoarsely, "And will you please sit down!"

"The appointment's in fifteen minutes mum, and we don't know where it is!"

"Oh, I hadn't realised. I'm sorry sweetheart. We can ring them and make it later."

"No, no, we can't!" I howled. "Please mum!"

She was getting embarrassed. "He's coming back, sit down!"

Neil, who was weaving his way between the tables, had obviously overheard us.

"Anything wrong?" he asked, sliding back into the booth and placing his hand over my mother's.

"No, nothing" she smiled, "Louise missed an appointment – but we can reschedule, can't we Louise?"

It was hopeless. I couldn't argue with her in front of her date.

"Yes mum."

Vaguely aware that a battle had been fought in his absence – a battle of which he was, somehow, the victor, Neil picked up his wallet with an air of great importance, and tucked it into the breast pocket of his suit. "Well then, that's settled. Why don't I take you for some ice-cream?"

It was still warm when we boarded the ferry. Mum made straight for the upper decks. "Let's stand where we were before. There's a nice view from there. And I'm dying for a ciggie! It is a pain when they don't smoke!" I followed her and said nothing. The sun, a little muted now, shone lazily on my back, warming my skin as the ferry cut its way easily through the calm and glassy water. The harbour was essentially a cove, its mouth shaped by two strips of cliff known as North and South Head. South Head had become a popular spot for gangs of drunken youths retreating from the police; and had, through numerous misadventures, earned the title Suicide Point. I kept my eyes fixed upon the narrow maw of the bay, trying to imagine the view from those cliffs. Beyond the cove could be glimpsed fuel tankers and fishing boats, going about their business on the open ocean. There were always half a dozen out there, sailing up and down the coast. At night, their safety lights on and swinging with the tide, the distant tankers would cease to be salt bitten oil vessels, melting instead into decorative beads of light that pierced the darkness here and there, furtively tracing the horizon.

I was bereft. Still stunned by the betrayal, but thawing from the shock that had silenced me earlier, I searched my mother's face – not really sure of what I was looking for. Perhaps I was waiting for her to say something apologetic – some recognition of what I had been forced to give up. As angry as I was, I had not the heart to ask for it. She looked sad. Her eyes were pinned to the water and the smile, fixed firmly all afternoon, had now vanished. The date had not gone well. She hadn't liked him - that was obvious (to me at least), towards Neil she had been the perfect lady. Mum had said nothing, but I knew she'd never see him again and his name would not be mentioned.

"Well," she sniffed, feigning cheer; "It's a day out isn't it?"

As the ferry steered towards Manly, I continued to stare at the narrowing gap between the two cliffs until it finally fell from sight. Here we were, safely hemmed in; making our way from one place to the other, separated only by an ocean from what I dreamed of as a vast and laden world – a world of which I'd never known and yet pined for with an urgency I could not suppress. Would I miss it? Would it pass by me, as the tankers did, just out of reach? I was determined that it wouldn't, that I wouldn't let fate, or luck, or circumstance confound me as it had today. This was to have been my day, the day on which I received the key to that other world. Instead I had returned from my adventure, granted only the realization that there was no key, no safe passage into a new and happier life; I should have to fight for it - and with that came the understanding that I might fail.

The water about us began to churn as if being brought to the boil. The ferry's ancient engine had been thrust into reverse and we were pulling into Manly Wharf. On the single, concrete covered limb that stretched towards us, tourists stood looking enviably languid amidst the tired and tight-lipped early evening's commuters. Holidaymakers and money-makers, each on their own adventure in what I believed the adult world to be, a place of choice and opportunity - enjoying a liberty I had yet to experience; I wasn't sure which of them I should envy most. The fact is I envied them all: everyone who wasn't me.

Once more I scanned the bay in search of its exit, but saw only rock face. One day, I thought, I will explore it. I will shed my clothes and disappointments. I will dive into the water and swim out into the ocean, to a world beyond the cove.

Her Last Words

Her last words were "Take the fruitcake with you." I don't know what to make of that. Did she know already that that was what she'd do? Maybe if I had left the cake there, she would have cut her self a thick slice of it and revelled in the tastes and textures of the crystallised fruits and stodgy dough, marvelling at life's little pleasures. Is that what she'd forgotten - that life has little pleasures? They are few and far between perhaps, but they are there.

No, she could not eat cake. What did she do instead? Go to the window, open the drapes and look over London, thinking that this clear, windy day was perfect to be her last? She may have cried for a while, for hours perhaps, tearing at her hair and her clothes, cursing the world, cursing herself - or me, cursing me. Did she hate me right there at the end, for not understanding her, for not being there, for not knowing that she shouldn't be left alone? Did she spit out my name like phlegm as she rocked herself to sleep surrounded by little brown plastic bottles? They tell me there had been hundreds: painkillers, sedatives - a veritable dolly mixture of chemicals. She must have squirreled them away in draws and cabinets, hidden beneath knickers or sitting innocently beside the dandruff shampoo we never used; waiting for the day she knew beyond a doubt that life and love were empty promises.

Licence to Drive

"I absolutely refuse! You, drive? You wouldn't last ten minutes! Do you know how difficult it is? For God's sake woman, I take you wherever you want to go, don't I? Well, don't I?"

Elisabeth focused on the vein in her husband's temple, tracing its shape snaking out from behind the hairline like a viper moving silently beneath sand. She was fascinated by the thought of the angry creature hidden there and imagined its scaly head bursting through the skin with jaws stretched like a sock puppet, exposing soft pink cushions of flesh and fangs as slim as fish bones.

"Bloody hell, you're not even listening!" Jim had turned almost purple now. Elisabeth said nothing; she knew full well that silence was her only option, having learnt very early in their marriage not to confront him. Jim's anger was easily aggravated and would sometimes escalate to the point that it took on an unearthly madness, as unfocused as it was intense. Six foot tall, Jim could cut quite a fearsome figure in his blacker moods. He was broad – not fat but square shouldered – with thick black hair that he parted fashionably to one side and a substantial, rather beaked nose. James Sinclair was not a good looking man but possessed a degree of charm that he used to good effect. It was with wit and charm that he had first wooed Elisabeth; now it seemed to her that there was little evidence left of the man she had fallen in love with – the warm, sincere man who had stood for an hour in the rain with an umbrella, waiting for her at the staff entrance of Brown's simply to ensure her dry passage home.

"God damn it, I'm going out for a drink! Put this behind you, do you hear me? I won't have it, simply won't have it!"

Elisabeth stood passively in the middle of the living room watching her husband move about her, gathering his things. Only when she had heard Jim slam the door behind him and seen through the window, his stubborn, solid figure march along the driveway did Elisabeth allow herself to blink, pressing out a tear that spilled across her cheek. She heard an engine start: he was taking the car, "Probably just to spite me" she thought.

The Lamb and Flag, Jim's weekday local, stood at the top of Kite Hill: a rough patch of land reached by a snicket that ran alongside their back garden. Throughout the summer children would fly their kites there, squealing and squawking through the long grass. In winter it became a toboggan run, its steep, snowy slope perfect for the flattened cardboard boxes that the youngsters fashioned into makeshift sleighs. Footpaths bordered both sides, each meandering up to the village; at the top of the nearest path stood the pub – less than a five minute walk from the house when the weather was fine.

Her eyes still closed, Elisabeth saw the image of her husband (as she had done many times, sat beside him in her role as patient passenger) climb into the driver's seat and with his left hand, wiggle the gear stick whilst guiding the key in his right smoothly through the lock. There was such authority in the way that sharp twist of his wrist could command an engine to splutter into action. Reluctant or not it would always obey him, just as she did – just as the whole world appeared to. There was something about Jim that instilled awe in the people who encountered him; even his mother had seemed timid of him the few times they'd gone to visit.

Elisabeth was his second wife; she had been only fifteen when they had met and Jim, thirty. He had swept her off her feet with a mixture of charm and fatherliness that had both reassured and impressed her. Elisabeth was the youngest child of seven in a traditional catholic family fraught with all of the guilt and mixed values typical of their faith. In contrast to her mother, who was the mouthpiece of the family with a sharp tongue and quick hand, her father was a gentle man, kind and quiet and had adored all of his children, finding much solace from them. Although (for fear of hurting anyone's feelings) he would never have admitted it, Elisabeth knew that she had been his favourite and had it not been for the lack of kindness in her mother's love and her father's timidity in voicing his opinion, she would probably have been there still, nestled in the safety of her childhood home. When Jim had started courting Elisabeth, her mother had been pleased; her youngest daughter did not seem much of a match for the tall, imposing man who came to visit but, she had reasoned, he obviously cared for the girl and would give her a better future than she could ever forge for herself. The truth was Elisabeth's mother was tired of parenting and more than ready to relinquish responsibility. "Thirty-two years of child rearing is enough," she had told her husband, "Let this one fend for her self - she's stubborn enough to manage!"

Elisabeth's father was unconvinced; he didn't like Jim, finding him arrogant and dismissive. He felt sorry for his little girl but had said nothing, knowing that, between her own misguided affection for the older man and his wife's determination to reclaim her freedom, Elisabeth stood little chance of escaping this marriage.

It had been a civil ceremony: Jim being atheist and refusing to humour any of Elisabeth's pleas for a church wedding. When she'd asked for a gown with a veil he had laughed at her, genuinely amused. "School girl rubbish Elisabeth! Completely unnecessary and wasteful and I will not, do you hear me, will not contemplate paying for several yards of netting my wife can only wear once!" In the end, she'd worn a borrowed pink woollen skirt with a matching tailored jacket and long white boots. Everyone had said how pretty she looked but, despite the bright smiles and photogenic poses, Elisabeth had been quietly devastated; she hadn't wanted to look pretty, it was her wedding day and she'd wanted to look like a princess. Two years on, the day had remained a bitter memory; eighteen years old with only a partly explored youth and a house bought by her father as a dowry, here she was, married to a man that she did not love and three months pregnant with his child. Elisabeth cast her thoughts back further to the naïve young teenager who had quickly graduated from shop assistant to window dresser at Brown's: it was Bradford's biggest department store and a job much sought after - how proud she had been! A blonde, blue-eyed beauty with long, lean limbs, Elisabeth had drawn as many faces to the window as the stiff limbed models she clothed, her features finer and skin more perfect than any of the mannequins with which she wrestled. Men and woman alike would stop to admire her, feigning interest in the season's new skirts and jackets on display. It was there that Jim had first seen her and come into the store to ask her out to dinner. Within three months he had persuaded her to stop working, promising her parents that their daughter would never have to work again. Elisabeth knew she was supposed to be grateful, but she wasn't. She had loved that job, the friends she had made there, the freedom of riding the bus into town each morning, the appreciative stares of the window gazers – and the memory that she had been good at something.

Minutes had passed and still she did not move from where she was standing. On the wall opposite was a large framed portrait: a photograph Jim had taken of her shortly after they'd met. Elisabeth found herself staring deep into the glass, past the soft skinned face that smiled back at her and into the shadowy reflection of the face she wore now. Two young women returned her gaze, one face full of life and expectancy, the other set in a sad expression of resignation. Elisabeth understood that both of the faces were hers and yet she felt she did not possess either of them, aware that she remained somehow apart, drifting between them - an impostor tenuously grasping the cord by which they were all linked. The recognition that somewhere she had misplaced herself brought with it a swell of nausea from deep in her gut. Elisabeth ran to the kitchen and threw up in the sink, bringing up the breakfast she had forced herself to eat that morning. She watched the putrid blend of eggs and toast slide towards the plughole and fought the urge to retch again; it was the second time she'd thrown up that day and the back of her throat burned. She reached for a glass and filled it with water, swilling each gulp thoroughly around her mouth before spitting it out. Elisabeth had been suffering from morning sickness since the eighth week and had grown accustomed to its symptoms; she felt the familiar surge of blood to her head and knew that she was about to become dizzy. "How will I cope?" she thought, pressing her palms into the smooth lip of the workbench to steady herself. "How will I get to the prenatal appointments? And buy baby clothes? And get the kid to school?" The thought of relying on Jim to take them everywhere filled Elisabeth with dread. By not allowing her to drive, Jim had placed Elisabeth in the unnerving position of having to ask his permission almost every time she left the house. Their street was a cul-de-sac, ten minutes walk from the village and at least twenty minutes drive to Shipley's town centre; the only way Elisabeth could shop was when Jim drove her there on the weekends. It meant that everything she bought – even her clothing, was under the watchful eye of her husband. Elisabeth couldn't remember the last time she'd actually worn a blouse that she liked; Jim's taste being far more sombre than her own, he often chose for her soft, muted colours and styles that made Elisabeth feel like a middle-aged woman. Once, when they had first begun shopping together, she had told him this and he had glared at her accusingly. "Would you rather look like a floozy?" he had asked in a cold, low voice. The look had genuinely scared Elisabeth and she had shaken her head slowly, swallowing any urge to respond. They had bought the blouses in silence and she worn them without protest, hiding in a suitcase on top of the wardrobe, the brighter, bolder outfits she had brought with her from home - remnants of a brief era between schoolgirl and housewife when she had truly been herself.

That night, Jim returned later than usual and went straight up to bed. He could hear the TV and knew Elisabeth was still in the living room but didn't stop to say goodnight from the hallway as he normally would. He was still mad at her, her demand for independence sitting heavily on his shoulders all evening - so much so that neither ale nor whisky could lighten him. Three months pregnant and nagging about driving herself around; inconceivable! How could she think of trying to cope without him? Could she not see that he had to be responsible for her? A vulnerable young woman, as much a child as a wife, could not be set free to roam at will with neither protection nor guidance. Left ungoverned, how then could she remain the innocent creature he loved? He knew that wasn't something he should think; it was the sixties, these were modern times with men and women working beside one another in factories and offices. But, he reasoned, these were women of the world like his first wife Betty. That had been a mistake he had no wish to repeat. Betty had turned out to be rather ambitious: after four years of marriage he had come home from work one day to find her sitting in the living room of their small flat looking sombre and tearful. She'd offered no real explanations; all she had said was that she had outgrown him (and then had left the next day to take up a secretarial position in Doncaster). Jim sat on the edge of the bed and began to unlace his shoes, trying to suppress the memory. The shoes were getting old, he noted; the winter had bitten into them, the soft Italian leather never being intended to suffer Yorkshire's inclement weather. "Things wear out so quickly nowadays." he thought ruefully, tucking them under the bed. Elisabeth was everything to him; precious indeed but not bright, it had to be said, not calculating; she could hurt herself, hurt his child. She could forget what the gears did, which one was the brake and which the clutch. She could panic and smash into one of the dry stone walls that map the lonely roads of the moors and be lost to him. She could leave; it had suddenly occurred to him that, with or without his permission, one day - any day, she could leave. And it was this one single thought had plagued him all evening. With a weary sigh he heaved his legs on to the bed and lay back to contemplate the ceiling. "Maybe if I encourage her to decorate one of the rooms. After all, we will need a nursery." he mused, "She'd like that – yes, a project. I could take her to the store on Saturday to look at wallpaper, find a nice pattern to brighten things up." Satisfied with this decision, Jim rolled on to his side, preparing for sleep. "I won't mention it just yet" was his final thought; "She'll probably see sense in the morning."

Downstairs in the living room, Elisabeth was planning. The television unnoticed, blared music at her; Ready Steady Go was on (a repeat of a previous episode) and an unknown rock band strutted their stuff on a stage surrounded by jostling teenagers. Elisabeth did not see them; she had her head down staring at the set of keys resting in her palm. They were the spare keys to the car that Jim kept on a hook in the kitchen; she'd taken them down hours earlier and put them in her pocket not really knowing why. Now, in her hand they felt hot and strangely heavy, weighted with intent and the concentration with which Elisabeth stared at them. "Tomorrow is Tuesday," she thought. She knew Jim's colleague David, would pick him up at eight the next morning: the men took turns to drive into Bradford together, enjoying the chance to socialise before they started their day's work. "Tomorrow," she whispered, her own quiet voice masked by the music, "Jim will be at work all day and the car will be here. Tomorrow I will learn to drive."

Jim left at eight as planned. They had not spoken that morning, Elisabeth feigning sleep until the moment she'd heard the front door close. Dressing quickly, she went downstairs to the kitchen and made herself a cup of tea. The keys were back on the hook, Elisabeth having put them there just before going to bed. The last thing she needed was Jim noticing their disappearance; he would put two and two together very quickly and then all hell would break loose. Elisabeth knew that she had to be careful, she didn't know how long it would take her to learn the gears and pedals and so forth, having never before attempted it, but she was aware that she may have to maintain the deceit for a while. The thought both frightened and thrilled her; amongst the maelstrom of fears crowding Elisabeth's mind she heard the echo of someone familiar – the voice of the defiant young woman she had searched for in her reflection the day before; it was nice to know that despite Elisabeth's fears she was still there.

Picking up the keys, Elisabeth let the voice guide her out of the house and down the driveway, bringing her to a standstill beside the car. It was a blue Ford with chrome wing mirrors and a shallow domed bonnet. One key was for the boot, the other for the door, Elisabeth did not know which was which but chose one and allowed herself a smile when it slipped easily into the lock. It was quiet on the street but she looked carefully around her anyway, knowing that she could not afford to be seen. A passing remark by a neighbour in the street or at the pub could give her away and Elisabeth dreaded the thought of Jim's finding out what she'd been up to. Of course he would have to know at some point – but not until she was ready. Sitting in the driver's seat, Elisabeth stared down at the pedals; Jim had told her once what each of them did. At the time she'd smiled sweetly as though only half interested and then watched him the rest of the journey out of the corner of her eye, pressing his left foot down each time he changed gear and extending his right each time they pulled away from a traffic light.

The only problem was that this morning the car stood facing the garage, away from the street: Elisabeth would have to reverse it. Turning the key in the lock she took a deep, long breath and depressed the clutch; it took her a couple of minutes to manoeuvre the gear stick in the direction marked 'R' on its black, spherical knob but she found it eventually. Releasing the handbrake and shifting the weight of her feet as evenly as she could from left to right, she felt the seat vibrate beneath her and the crunching sound of tyres on gravel as the car slowly moved backwards. A second later it stopped, cutting out with a violent clunk, jolting Elisabeth forward. She pressed her foot down on the clutch and turned the key again. Once more the car lurched into life and instantly continued its reverse crawl onto the street. Many times, Elisabeth had watched Jim pull the wheel smoothly to the left as he did this, sliding the car around to face the cul-de-sac's exit; Elisabeth did the same until, switching her right foot to the middle pedal, she brought the car to a ragged halt. Again it cut out and again Elisabeth put her foot on the clutch and turned the key, this time gliding the gear into neutral. She knew first was somewhere to the left but each time she pressed the accelerator the car's engine let out a futile roar, unable to move forward. Shifting the gear stick back into neutral, Elisabeth stared intently at the knob, trying to relate the subtle difference in position between the numbers one and three. "It's just practice," she thought, wiggling the stick with the palm of her hand just as she'd seen Jim do. "You can do this Beth!" She had no choice; now that she had got the car out of the drive, she'd have to put it back again somehow or Jim would know and that would be the end of it, she'd never have another chance. Pressing the stick once more to the left, she guided it into first and felt with pleasure the pull of the tyres as the car shuffled forward. After an unsuccessful attempt to pull the seat closer to the pedals, with her body perched precariously on its edge and the trim cutting into her thigh, Elisabeth drove slowly around the large grassy island that formed the cul-de-sac's central roundabout.

All those years she'd been a passenger in first her father's, then her husband's car and yet Elisabeth was sure she'd never experienced before the sensation of gliding that now entranced her.

There were two telegraph poles protruding from the grassy islet and Elisabeth imagined the car winding an invisible thread around them, guiding her round. By the twelfth circuit Elisabeth felt she'd had enough; she wondered what the two slim wands on either side of the wheel were for and wanted to park so that she could explore them. After manoeuvring the car back into the driveway, taking care to leave it in the same place she'd found it, Elisabeth pulled back the handbrake and switched off the engine. The curious pair of joysticks temporarily forgotten, she sat for a moment, her hand resting consciously upon the small bulge of her belly. Suddenly she felt exhausted – but also remarkably lucid, as if the enormity of what she was doing had finally hit her. The clock in the dashboard read ten past nine; it was still early. If she started the laundry straight away she could have the house tidied and sheets hung out by twelve. "That would give me time to have another go this afternoon." Elisabeth thought. The earlier the better; Jim wouldn't be back until six but the neighbourhood children, who finished school at three thirty, would be scattered across the street by four, tearing about on their bicycles. Elisabeth couldn't risk being seen and innocent youngsters, she knew, often made dangerous gossips, twittering at their parents in an endless monologue of what they'd done and who they'd seen, throwing questions like darts about any and every small thing that struck them as odd. Elisabeth could just imagine it. "Mummy, why was that blonde lady from number 14 driving around in circles all afternoon – was she lost?" It would only take one naïve comment carried back to Jim to cause havoc. How did she know that someone hadn't already seen her? Elisabeth felt dread rise in her throat; any one of her neighbours could have been looking out of their window that morning and seen her pass. The car was new and enviably distinctive in comparison to those normally seen parked on the cul-de-sac. She would be easily recognised. "There's no point worrying about it now," she decided stoically, getting out of the car. It had taken Elisabeth months to work up the courage to do this; and now she had. The realisation thrilled her but she dampened it instantly. "There's a lot more to learn," she thought soberly, once more reaching for her swollen stomach, "And not a lot of time."

It had rained earlier: as a warm afternoon sun peeked between the clouds Elisabeth searched the sky for signs of a rainbow. Seeing none she contented herself with counting the fuzzy white shapes dotting the hillside; from a distance, the grazing sheep looked to her like cotton wool balls. Jim had remained silent for most of the journey. They'd had Sunday lunch at a pub in Keighley (the roast at the Lamb and Flag being often a little overcooked for Jim's taste and miserly in portion) and after lunch they had driven up to the moors for a short walk. He'd noticed then that the petrol gauge was running low, in spite of the fact that he'd filled the tank only two days before on his way home from work. He'd been called in to the office again on Saturday; there had been an urgent job on and David had also been called in so Jim had ridden in with him. How, he wondered, could the car have used so much petrol? He glanced across at Elisabeth sitting quietly beside him. She had been rather distant these past few months (but thankfully much calmer than she had been in the spring). Perhaps, he reasoned, she was becoming more content at the prospect of being a mother. "Women like children," he thought. They seemed to handle them with much more ease than men, holding them with a capable nonchalance that men's large hands and burly movements could never seem to muster. He hadn't particularly wanted children. Of course, he had nothing against them personally - it was just that, despite their cute appearance, they seemed mostly to get under foot as babies and later under your skin with showers of non-sequiturs and loudly squealed questions. However, Jim had to concede that this baby's conception had been no accident. He'd realised soon after their marriage that his bride was far more headstrong than he'd given her credit for; it quickly became obvious to him that Elisabeth needed something to ground her – some sense of responsibility. Jim had not felt the need to discuss this with Elisabeth: she rarely seemed to know what she wanted, flipping from one ideal to another. The poor girl truly believed that had she a dozen lives to live (and the opportunity to spend them as she pleased) she would have been a hairdresser, a model, make-up artist – or designer, no less! He couldn't help but chuckle at the disparate jumble of vocations she assumed quixotically were within her grasp.

Elisabeth turned to look at him. "What are you thinking about?" she asked him innocently.

"Ah, the epitome of confusion!" he mused, relishing his own mirth. "Not a thing my dear," he said, "Not a thing."

Elisabeth had noticed Jim staring at the petrol gauge and seen his brow furrow. "Please God!" she prayed silently, "Please don't let him notice!" It had never occurred to her that, after all her efforts to conceal her actions over the last few months, she could be betrayed by something as simple as by the dial on a fuel gauge. Why hadn't she thought of it? Of course, from now on she would have to start filling up the tank. "Where will I get the money?" she wondered dismally. She had none of her own and Jim only gave her enough housekeeping each week to cover the few things that needed replenishing between shopping trips, such as bread and milk. There was another problem: Elisabeth had never used a petrol pump before; she'd have to ask the attendant for help. Where would she find a garage close to home where she wouldn't be recognised? Jim was well known in the area; almost every time she'd been with him when he'd stopped for petrol, Elisabeth had been left to sit waiting in the car whilst he had chatted with one of the mechanics that always seemed to be loitering on the forecourts, smoking cigarettes. Being quite an enthusiast on the subject, Jim would banter with them on the best way to recondition one part of the engine or another. If they didn't recognise her, they were bound to recognise the car. Elisabeth felt her throat flush with panic and tugged at the collar of her coat so that it brushed against her cheeks.

"Are you cold?" Jim asked her, looking genuinely concerned. His obvious worry touched her and she smiled.

"Not too much."

Suddenly the whole masquerade seemed foolish. "I'll tell him tonight" she thought. "I can sit with him and explain how important it is with the baby coming that I'm able to get to the shops, the doctor's or, God forbid, the hospital! He'll understand." But deep in her heart she knew he wouldn't. She was young perhaps but not completely stupid. Her husband had no intention of slackening the reigns; he didn't trust her – and with good reason she had to admit. A licence to drive was licence to leave; Jim knew it, they both knew it. Elisabeth also knew that time was running out. She was six months pregnant. "If I am actually going to take the test" she thought, "I'll have to do it soon."

Elisabeth's recent adventures had had a remarkable effect on her; in spite of the increasing weight she had to bear, her complexion was no longer pale and her many short walks on the moors had left subtle traces of sunshine in her hair. Spring that year had been glorious. After a week of circumventing the roundabout, she had figured out the gears and had soon ventured out of the cul-de-sac into the surrounding streets of Baildon. The first time she'd driven through the village Elisabeth had been terrified of being seen and had worn a headscarf, knotted like a farmer's wife under the chin. She needn't have worried: nobody, it seemed, took a blind bit of notice in the cars that drove past. Burdened with shopping bags, their gaze fixed solidly on the skittish offspring who darted to and fro ahead of them; it was as if their world stopped at the edge of the pavement. Elisabeth had carried on driving out of the village and onto the moors. April's pale sun had made the undulating hills seem liquid somehow, milky and undefined like a watercolour painting. Elisabeth had parked the car and wound down the window, relishing for once her solitude. At home, her isolation had been claustrophobic, her life and its boundaries dictated by a prison of red brick and wallpapered walls. Outside it was different; be it sitting in the car or wandering across moorland, Elisabeth discovered that there was freedom to be found in being alone. She had driven up to the moors many times throughout the summer. As the weather had got warmer and the hills more verdant, Elisabeth had grown to appreciate more the wondrous countryside that lapped at the perimeters of Yorkshire's grimy, bustling towns.

  She had been born in Bradford and raised on one of the numerous council estates making up its suburbs. A regular two up, two down, it was a tight squeeze for a family of nine, but they had managed. One by one her brother and sisters had found jobs and moved out. (Only Patricia the eldest had, like Elisabeth, departed a newly wed.) By the time she had turned twelve there had been just herself and her parents; all the noise and playfulness had vanished from the house and life had gradually become still (still meaning stagnant in the eyes of a child). Weekdays had been even lonelier than weekends: the convent school that Elisabeth had attended followed a strict, unforgiving curriculum with corporal punishment seen as an essential teaching tool. The nuns' fondness for snapping a wooden ruler across 'lazy' hands when they felt that the pupil's letter construction or spelling required greater attention had left Elisabeth with sore knuckles most days of the week. She had never been a good speller and had developed a deep fear of reading, never quite able to make sense of the words in front of her. The longer she focused on them, trying to shift the patterns into something familiar, the more they eluded her. In spite of her timid attempts to explain this phenomenon to her parents and teachers, it had simply been assumed by everyone that the pretty young teenager was stupid and Elisabeth had been repeatedly encouraged to leave school and to find work of some kind.

  "Nothing too complex though" her mother had told her, "You'd be of no use to anyone in an office – maybe service or telephone work would suit you better."

There had been no maybe about it: Elisabeth's mother had already formulated a plan. That morning a neighbour had mentioned to her that a department store in town was taking on shop assistants in preparation for the Christmas rush. That same afternoon, she had announced that she'd rung the store's personnel department and booked an interview; Elisabeth was expected at ten the following day.

"You won't necessarily have to handle money or work the cash register," her mother had added cheerfully, "They have lots of openings for floor staff. Hard on the feet but I'm sure you'll get used to it."

Elisabeth had sat looking acquiescent, absorbing everything being said with quiet glee. She had always understood that though they loved her, her parents had little faith in her ability to extend herself. This was more than she could have hoped for: rather than being forced to take a job as a receptionist – or worse still as a café waitress, Elisabeth had been given the opportunity to work surrounded by what she loved most: clothes!

"Of course" she had reasoned later that night, lying awake with excitement, "It's not going to be glamorous - but at least I won't get scalded every morning, serving bacon and eggs to lorry drivers!"

She had passed the interview with ease, her chirpy manner impressing the stout, middle-aged manager who (more than a little distracted by the coy smile and slim legs of the young blonde sat across from him) had not asked for her academic records nor questioned her too fiercely on her suitability for such a position.

Her well rehearsed responses unneeded, Elisabeth had left his office assured of being taken on and had bought herself a currant teacake with which to celebrate before catching the bus home.

Their journey back from lunch in Keighley had been quite pleasant, with Elisabeth responding to Jim's kindness and concern with a sudden urge to confess her secret. Luckily she had held her tongue: within minutes of arriving home Jim noticed that his shirts for the week were still crumpled in the washing basket, damp and entangled. Elisabeth had meant to hang them out before they'd set off that morning but in the rush to be ready on time had forgotten. She watched helplessly as Jim snatched them one by one out of the basket, holding them aloft for scrutiny, as if there were a jury present.

"And what am I supposed to wear in the morning?" he bellowed at her, his face twisted with rage. "This one?" he added, stabbing his chest with his finger.

Tired from the drive and utterly bewildered at his change in behaviour, Elisabeth responded without thinking, telling him frankly that she'd often left out the same shirt for him three days in a row, proving that he didn't actually know the difference between a clean shirt and a dirty one. In one violent gesture, Jim flung the shirts at her, "Get these sorted out!"

"All you wear is white!" she yelled at his back as he stormed from the kitchen. "Your shirts are as boring as the rest of you!"

There was no response; instead silence and then the sickening crack of brittle plastic. Elisabeth realised instantly what he had done and flew into the sitting room to find her husband stood holding two halves of a black vinyl disc; it was one of the several long playing records that she kept beside the gramophone. (The rest she kept hidden knowing that Jim would scald her for wasting money.)

"How could you?" she whispered, disbelievingly.

Jim levelly returned her stare, his blank expression bearing no trace of remorse. "Too much time spent on silly things" he said, his voice devoid of any tone, then turned and left the room, still gripping the record in the manner with which he'd snapped it - one miserable, jagged piece in each hand.

Elisabeth sank wearily onto the settee, still shocked and unable to make sense of the spiteful destruction she had just witnessed. "I can't believe I was actually going to tell him" she thought, casting her mind back to their warm exchange in the car and the brief moment of tenderness that had almost entrapped her. "Well, not now," she vowed vehemently beneath her breath, staring coldly at the man who stood proudly beside her in the wedding photograph that sat on top of the television. "Not now. In fact, if I can help it Jim, by the time you'll find out I'll be gone!"

It was one o'clock and Elisabeth had still not come to bed. Jim lay awake listening to the sounds of the house. Above him in the attic he could hear the cistern draining: she was running a tap somewhere. There had been no movement on the stairs and none in the bathroom so he assumed that she was in the kitchen. "Probably making more tea," he thought, "No wonder she can never sleep." He had not wanted to argue (it had ruined a perfectly nice day) but her carelessness had really irked him. Elisabeth was constantly misplacing things and could never recall a telephone message correctly, always giving him the wrong name or confusing information. More than once he had missed a doctor or dentist's appointment due to Elisabeth noting down the wrong date or mishearing two o'clock as twelve. It was inconceivable to him that anyone should find such things confusing. How on earth, he wondered, was she going to cope with the child - but then dismissed the thought; how hard can it be? What brains does it take to dress, feed, and care for something? It would be fine, he decided - young women did it all the time. Elisabeth was finally coming to bed. Jim could hear the stairs' small boards creak underfoot as she made her way up. He glanced again at the alarm clock on his bedside table; it was one-thirty. He hoped that, at the very least, she'd hung his shirts up properly; he'd have to iron one himself in the morning. "I suppose I can't ask her to get up and do it" he reasoned begrudgingly, "After all, she is pregnant."

Sat on the edge of the bath in her nightdress, Elisabeth stared dolefully down at the lurid pink matt beneath her feet. There was a matching piece tucked neatly around the base of the toilet. "Who bought these things?" she wondered incredulously.

They had got numerous wedding presents; all the things that newlyweds need for building a home together. These things now littered the house, adorning floors and table tops or sat in kitchen cupboards waiting to be useful. Elisabeth, though at the very epicentre of its construction, felt she'd had no hand in any of it: the world in which she now existed had been built up around her by other people. From the second she had agreed to marry Jim, she had known she was not ready – not ready for marriage, not ready for homemaking and certainly not ready for children. The fear of disappointing her parents, of hurting Jim, of being cast out in shame by those she relied on, had silenced her. Well trained for martyrdom by her family's faith (and lack of faith in her) Elisabeth had said yes because she felt she must; now, the dutiful wife and soon to be mother, Elisabeth questioned bitterly why it had fallen upon her rather than one of her elder siblings, to be groomed for immolation.

Once, during a childhood argument, her brother David, in a fit of sibling vitriol, had called her the runt of the family, saying that, had they been a litter of puppies, their parents would have drown her at birth. Never more than at this moment did she feel it to be true.

"You idiot Elisabeth," she cursed aloud, "I will take care of you, he says. Trust me, he says, so you do - you bleeding fool!"

Throughout the entirety of their courtship, when questioned, Jim's attitude to children had been one of reluctance and so Elisabeth had believed him when he had said he would always be careful when they made love. He had used protection most of the time and when there was none, had always taken extra care – or so she had thought. Sex to Elisabeth was a realm previously unexplored and as confusing and mysterious to her as the adult world in general. She had lived a sheltered existence in so many ways; much younger than the rest of her siblings, Elisabeth had missed out on the banter and propaganda that had spread between her sisters, educating them on the manner of men. Her mother, dour and devout in her dealings with her, had told her nothing, proclaiming that her future spouse would one day enlighten Elisabeth on the ways of the world. By the time Elisabeth had found out what these ways were, she was revelling in the attention of courtship, thinking she was in love. When given nothing with which to compare them, the most of modest pleasures seem marvellous at first. Now there was no pleasure, she concluded – only consequence, a child she did not want and a future mapped out for her in a loveless union with a man becoming more of a stranger to her everyday. He would be asleep by now, she reasoned, his slow uneven breaths punctuated by guttural snores. They had been happy, she told herself; they had laughed and danced and spoken in soft whispers late into the night, sat on her mother's couch. Wasn't that something close to love?

Picking up the clothes she'd changed out of, Elisabeth put them in the washing basket and went out onto the landing. She paused just outside the bedroom, her ear against the white-gloss door, listening for the telltale wheezes within. "Please be asleep," her mind pleaded with him, "Please, please be asleep." Turning the handle as quietly as she could, Elisabeth opened the door slowly and stepped stealthily into the room. She realised immediately that Jim was still awake; she could feel his eyes upon her, searing through the darkness.

"Elisabeth? Finally. Are you coming to bed?"

"Yes." she answered, her heart plummeting as she slipped between the sheets.

Jim was out of the house by seven-thirty the next morning having found his shirt neatly pressed and hung on the back of a chair in the kitchen. From behind the bedroom window's voile curtains, Elisabeth watched his car pull out of the driveway and onto the cul-de-sac; she waited until he had disappeared from view then finished dressing and went downstairs to make herself a cup of tea. Sitting up the night before waiting for Jim's shirt to dry over on the radiator, Elisabeth had come to a decision: she would take the test as soon as possible, whether or not she was ready. It had also occurred to Elisabeth that she couldn't manage it alone, she would have to confide in someone; there was only one person she could trust: Margot.

In childhood, Margot had been Elisabeth's best friend; they had spent most of their school-lives together, bonding under the sufferance of convent oppression and had dreamed of a glorious adulthood in each other's company, sharing not just a flat but also a glamorous existence as girls about town, freed from the religious restraints of their childhood. Borne of rather more liberal parents, Margot had indeed gone on to do just that, achieving what her dear friend could not: life on her own terms. Although envious, Elisabeth felt no resentment towards Margot – in fact she felt nothing but awe for the woman her friend had grown up to become. Margot was tenacious in all the ways that Elisabeth was not; more precocious than her friend, Margot had gaily danced her way into (and out of) numerous courtships, rejecting several proposals of marriage along the way. At life's crossroads, where Elisabeth had stood and brooded, Margot had battled on; everything about their characters and lifestyles were so disparate – it amazed Elisabeth that they were still friends at all. It had been a long time since they'd spoken, almost a year in fact. Soon after discovering she was pregnant, Elisabeth had rung the number Margot had given her when they'd last spoken but had got no response and so had called Margot's mother, asking her to pass on the news. Margot's mother had told her that Margot had taken a summer job as a tour operator in Italy but planned to return in the autumn.

"July I think, dear. But the next time she calls me, I will tell her the good news – I won't forget!" she had assured Elisabeth kindly.

Since then Elisabeth had heard nothing and as she sat drinking her tea she chewed on the thought that Margot, who would have been back in England for several weeks now, might not want to speak to her. Jim's increasing possessiveness had made maintaining her friendship with Margot difficult. The last time she'd seen her had been during the January sales; Jim had dropped Elisabeth off outside the coffee shop in Bradford, instructing her to be in the same spot three hours later so that he could take her home. Margot was a keen shopper and she and Elisabeth had spent the afternoon trawling the town centre's many department stores in search of bargain priced accessories. They'd returned to the coffee shop half an hour early so that the two of them could warm up and have a last natter before Jim arrived. The hot, milky coffee they drank had re-invigorated them and their conversation; it wasn't until an hour later, when Elisabeth had glanced up and saw Jim's scowling face searching for her from the doorway, that she realised she'd lost track of time. Following Elisabeth's horrified gaze, Margot had turned to catch him glowering at them, his hands thrust into the pockets of his raincoat like a disgruntled foreman. "He looks annoyed doesn't he?" she'd giggled, "Beth, Are you going to be in trouble?" And then Margot had cheerfully called out to him, waving for him to come join them. Elisabeth had watched her husband walk towards the table with a purposeful step; "Oh God, he really does look angry," she'd thought, not savouring the journey home. Jim hadn't joined them but had stood instead at Elisabeth's shoulder, his six-foot frame seeming to loom over them, casting a shadow.

"I've been waiting for thirty minutes Elisabeth."

Margot had been unabashed, "Hello Jim, sorry about that. Once I get going I never stop."

By way of response, Jim had thrown her a gelid, condescending glance and then returned his attention to Elisabeth.

"I assume you're ready to go now?"

It had been a statement only thinly disguised as a question. Recognizing her husband's rhetoric, Elisabeth knew better than to answer and had quietly gathered her things, mumbling an apologetic farewell to her friend. Margot had watched them leave with a worried look on her face; it was obvious that Jim's behaviour had greatly unnerved her. He would be glad of that, he didn't like Margot - nor had he liked any of the girls at Brown's Elisabeth had briefly befriended before their marriage (and had taken little care in hiding it). "They're children!" he would growl at their very mention. "Silly creatures with silly thoughts that spill out in silly sentences!"

And so Elisabeth had learned not to mention them. When she'd first quit work, there had been numerous invitations to join them for drinks but Jim had always refused her requests for taxi fare and yet had seen no reason why he himself should drive her about 'at all hours of the night'. Tiring of Elisabeth's obviously concocted excuses not to socialise with them, one by one, the girls had stopped calling.

Her husband had scoffed at her friends' forsaking her. "You've no need of people like that. We have plenty of friends!" But all of Jim's friends were older (much older in fact) and their wives invariably greeted her with disdain when she and Jim occasionally joined them for Sunday lunch at the local pub. Whilst the men chatted amiably the women would fire jibes at her, noting the immaturity of her opinions and the lack of panache in her clothes. Jim seemed oblivious to it and when Elisabeth had dared tearfully repeat their remarks on the way home one day, he had only smiled and informed her that they were jealous, that she was the prettiest wife in the village and therefore should expect a bit of resentment now and then.

"It's all about growing up love," he had said flatly, "Women are shallow creatures, there's not much more to them than hair and make-up."

When Elisabeth had related this back to Margot in one of their rare afternoon phone calls, her friend had laughed heartily.

"All hair and make-up we may be," she'd snorted, "But there's not a man alive on earth that who isn't thankful of it! Honestly Beth, that man has you in knots!"

Margot would help her; Elisabeth was sure she of it – that is if she could reach her. "Well" she concluded, draining the last of the tea from its cup, "There's only one way to find out." She walked through to the hallway where the telephone stood on a small ornate table with a chair beside it. Ignoring the chair, Elisabeth picked up the phone and sat cross-legged on the floor with it cradled in her lap. The receiver was cold against her ear as she dialled the number she had carefully copied into her address book almost a year earlier. Would Margot still live there, she wondered; she couldn't risk leaving another message with her mother knowing that Margot might call back when Jim was home. The phone rang out unanswered.

"What will I do now?" she pondered helplessly, wishing she'd thought of a contingency plan. "Just two more rings" she promised herself, lulled by the even purr of the ring tone.

"Hello?"

The voice made her jump. "Margot?" she asked hesitantly.

"Beth!" the voice responded with delight. "I was just thinking of you. Are you okay?"

For the first time in weeks, Elisabeth allowed herself a smile: her dear friend had not abandoned her after all and she felt the imagined gulf between them narrow instantly.

"No" she answered, too stressed and exhausted to be anything other than honest. "No I'm not okay – listen Margot, I really need your help."

Margot listened quietly to Elisabeth's dilemma and then, with all the pragmatism of a fairy godmother, told her that everything was going to be all right.

"We'll have you driving around town by Christmas sweetie" she reassured her. "Now hang up – I've got a couple of calls to make, I'll speak to you soon."

The hallway was cold: August winds pressed themselves against the ill-fitting front door, sneaking into the house as draughts that chilled the air around her. Elisabeth remained there a few minutes longer, uncertain as to what to do next. She left the phone on the floor but managed to pick herself up and then paced for a while from room to room under the guise of tidying up. Although it felt like a lifetime to Elisabeth, Margot called her back in less than an hour triumphant and excited, with an appointment booked for a fortnight later and an address in Bradford where Elisabeth would take the test. She'd even persuaded Derek, her brother, to lend them the car for the day.

"I just said I wanted it to move some stuff," she told Elisabeth. "You can't risk Jim taking yours on the very day you need it."

(Elisabeth enjoyed hearing Margot say yours as if the car could actually belong to her – it made the mammoth task ahead of her actually seem possible.)

"What you need to now Elisabeth is stay calm and practice as much as you can. Have you driven into town yet?"

Elisabeth had to admit that she hadn't; not only had she been worried that Jim or one of his colleagues would see her, Bradford's dual carriageways and complex traffic light systems still seemed a daunting prospect and Elisabeth had not been keen to tackle a fast moving river of other cars until she felt more confident of steering her way through and emerging from it safely.

"Well, you know what you've got to do," urged Margot.

"I know – and I will" Elisabeth promised.

"Right then, I'll see you on the tenth. I can't wait, we'll have a great day!"

Elisabeth felt tears rise to her throat. "Thank you Margot, thank you so much."

"Hey there, what are friends for?" And with that, Margot hung up leaving Elisabeth stiff limbed and in a state of bemusement, her unseeing gaze tracing the patterns on the hallway carpet.

The dining room clock had just chimed ten. Elisabeth, who had been up since seven, had cleaned the bathroom, devoured two bacon sandwiches and was on her fourth cup of tea when she heard the horn. She paused, listening for the agreed three honks; when the third sounded Elisabeth responded with a nervous shiver.

"Wow, it's really happening," she said aloud, gathering together her purse, her door key and a coat she'd already decided was much too warm to wear in the car but might be useful anyway. "Here we go!"

Margot sat at the wheel of a turquoise Morris Traveller, waiting at the mouth of the driveway with the car's engine running. As soon as she saw her she opened the door and leapt out to greet Elisabeth with a jubilant hug.

"Hello! My god, look at you – you're round!"

Elisabeth laughed, grateful for her much missed friend's enthusiasm and familiarity. "It is so good to see you – and thank you so much for this."

Margot swatted away her thanks with a well-manicured hand.

"Oh Beth, stop, it's a pleasure, it really is. I'm so proud of you!"

"However sweetie" she added in a serious voice, "We have forty-five minutes to get into Bradford and find this place. Hmm, mid-morning so there's still a fair bit of traffic."

Having thrown her bag and coat onto the backseat, Elisabeth was already climbing into the car; with a now sizeable bump to manoeuvre, it took her a few minutes to settle herself. Margot got back into the car laughing good-naturedly at her companions' pneumatic form and the evident discomfort it afforded her. "Are you ready?"

Elisabeth flashed her a weak, half-wincing smile. "Err, I think so!"

Margot retorted with a wink and a grin. "That'll do!" And then, with a confident flourish, Elisabeth's fairy godmother threw the car in reverse and swung out of the driveway with careless precision.

Elisabeth focused on her friend's profile as she talked of her travels and of Italian men as if landscape and physique were inexorably entwined. For once (having been barked at by Jim to do so on numerous occasions) facing reality seemed a happy adventure – a daunting task certainly, but not impossible. Elisabeth had no idea what trials lay ahead of her that day but in a rare moment of self-possession, bolstered by the nonchalant chatter of Margot beside her, she decided that it didn't matter, that having come this far and worked this hard, she would do nothing less than her best.

Margot bounced up and down, precariously wobbling the plastic chair on which she sat. "Come on, come on tell me! Stop being so blummin' coy!"

Elisabeth thought her friend might fall over at any second and reached out to steady her. "Well…"

"Argh! I can't stand it – and I want to go to the loo. Tell me now!"

Elisabeth giggled. "Okay, okay - yes."

"You passed?"

"Yes."

Margot's squeal was so shrill that it pierced every damp and austere corner of the licensing office, and did so fiercely; the other attendees looked on with mixed expressions of disgust and curiosity. Elisabeth laughed. "I'm glad you're happy"
"Happy?" her friend snorted, "I'm delirious Beth. I've been holding on for thirty minutes! Let's find a café – one with a toilet!"
Two cups of coffee and an Eccles cake later, the news had finally begun to sink in and Elisabeth related back to her friend the inspector's numerous comments on her driving. "He said my parking was awful."
Margot slurped her coffee, unimpressed. "Everyone's parking is awful Beth. Did he say anything good at all?"
"Yes" Elisabeth chirped happily.
"What?"
"I passed!"
The both of them giggled, pleased with the joke.
"Yep!" Margot chirped back, "That is pretty good."
Noticing darkness approach beyond the glass façade of the brightly lit café, Elisabeth glanced at her watch. "It's three o'clock already Margot. When did your brother want the car back?"
"Oh that's not a problem. We'd better get you home though I suppose – that is, if you want to be home before his majesty!"
Although she'd never openly encouraged them, Elisabeth savoured Margot's jibes at Jim. As witty as she was vocal in her irreverence of him, Margot lent an air of levity to Elisabeth's relationship that Elisabeth herself could never manage. She felt tired; winter was drawing in and the early sunset had made the day feel like a long one. Both women were quiet on the way back to Baildon, each lost in thoughts of their own. They arrived to see Jim's car in the driveway and a light on in the living room. Margot turned to her friend worriedly.
"He's back early isn't he? What are you going to tell him?"
Elisabeth shrugged and then cast Margot a wry smile. "I helped you move some stuff, remember?"
The friends exchanged goodbyes in the car, but before leaving Margot got out and hugged Elisabeth again who sensed that her friend was trying to bestow upon her some source of resolve.
"Now Beth, remember what we said, okay?"
"I will Margot, I promise."

"Take good care of yourself and that baby!" she called out the window as the car pulled away.

Elisabeth waved after her and then turned towards the house. Jim was at the window, watching her; she smiled, feigning nonchalance. He was in the kitchen, filling up the kettle, by the time she'd got to the back door.

"I saw Margot leaving. Where have you been?" he asked her

Elisabeth moved past him to the hallway to hang up her coat; she found it much easier to lie when he wasn't peering at her, trying to decode her expressions.

"She's just got back from working in Italy and needed a hand to move some things she'd left with her mother."

"Couldn't she have got one of her fancy men to do that for her?"

Elisabeth could hear the sneer in his voice but responded cheerfully, unwilling to aggravate him; she could tell Jim was poised for an argument.

"She doesn't have a fancy man; she's been away as I said. Anyway, it's done now. You're home early, everything okay?"

"No" he griped, "I feel awful. Damned canteen food! There was only beef curry on offer at lunch time – tasteless it was, and I've had a dickey stomach to thank for it all afternoon."

Jim watched his young wife move around the kitchen, fussing quietly over imaginary things. In spite of her present size, the girl appeared weightless – as if she might drift away the second he turned his back.

"I've put the kettle on," he said, his tone towards her unusually gentle.

Elisabeth stopped what she was doing, eyeing him warily through her fringe. "Thanks Jim, I'll make us some tea as soon as it's boiled."

She seemed distracted, Jim noted, and secretive - but then she often did. 'There's a world of dreams inside that woman' he mused, 'With no space for me in it.'

With their newborn son cradled carefully in her arms, Elisabeth followed Jim through the hall to the foot of the narrow staircase where she faltered. Jim did not stop or turn to look at her when she called out to him but carried on climbing the stairs.

"I'm shattered," she declared to his back, "Can't we have a cup of tea first?"

"No, come and see this, I promise you'll love it" he responded, disappearing onto the upstairs landing. With a sigh Elisabeth followed and found her husband in the spare bedroom, standing proudly beside an old non-descript wooden cot.

"Margery next door said we could have it. It's been sitting in her attic since her youngest, Tommy, grew out of it – he's four now, can you believe it? Anyway, I gave it a good wash. It looks as good as new doesn't it?"

Elisabeth could hear, not only in his self-congratulatory tone, but also by the excitement in his voice that Jim had put a lot of effort into this minor preparation for their homecoming. Although underwhelmed by the sight of the rickety piece of furniture in front of her, Elisabeth was grateful for Jim's warmth and enthusiasm - and this manly attempt at familial bonding. She looked down at the stirring bundle she was holding; the sense of loneliness that had consumed her as she'd nursed this tiny stranger at her breast on a cold dark ward the night before finally began to fade.

"It's perfect Jim, thank you."

Although far from perfect, Elisabeth knew it was naïve of her to have expected more. It would never have occurred to Jim to buy a new cot: her husband's penchant for cost cutting left no room for sentimentality or romanticism. Elisabeth had, throughout the pregnancy, begun to nurture an impression of not just the child's arrival but the wondrous array of accoutrements that the British Home Stores catalogue assured her accompanied it. Flicking through its pages Elisabeth had envisaged the colourful clothes and plastic toys spilling into every room, reinvigorating the house. Jim gestured glibly towards a corner of the small room where several open boxes stood; each one contained a jumble of magazines, desk ware and draughtsman's tools.

"I'll move those in the morning. Do you want a cup of tea?"

"Finally," thought Elisabeth. "I'd love one," she answered.

"Right then, tea it is!"

In a state of muted beatitude unusual of Jim's character, he briskly left the room and bounded downstairs, interrupting his stride only once to kiss Elisabeth tenderly on the forehead as he passed. Elisabeth took the baby over to the cot and inspected the bedding she found there. A soft cotton sheet clung to the slim foam mattress and though a little faded, the pale blue baby blanket was soft to the touch. "Good old Margery" Elisabeth murmured fondly. "And daddy hasn't done so badly either has he sweetheart?" she whispered to the dozing form as she laid him down gently, tucking the blanket loosely about his waist. On his back, with his arms spread and miniature hands clasped to reveal paper-thin nails and fragile wrists, her young son fell asleep utterly oblivious to the high bars surrounding him; Elisabeth, on the other hand, was not.

"Edward Arthur." Jim's voice rang out along the wood panelled corridor. Elisabeth was sitting sulkily on a bench a few feet away: she had argued vehemently with Jim over naming the baby Edward. "It's old and it's stuffy," she had protested, "And there are so many nice names now – Luke, Mark…"//
Jim had thrown his arms up in disgust. "What the hell are you trying to do? Turn him into a disciple? I'm not having you squeezing religion in to this family! Bloody Catholics!"
That hadn't even occurred to Elisabeth who had just liked the names.
"What about Jack?" She inquired hopefully. "Jack's nice."
"Not a chance!"
Determined that his son should have a strong, solid name that reflected the stoicism of English life, Jim had refused to debate the matter any further and on the way to the town hall the next day had sat in the car with his wife, silent and self-righteous. It was after all his decision, he reasoned; Elisabeth wasn't even capable of filling in the paperwork (he had taken great pleasure in pointing that out to her) and he was damned if he would scribe the letters J-a-c-k knowing that his firstborn would have to bear that frivolous name for the rest of his life – the child might not care but the man wouldn't thank him for it.
"It's a father's duty," he had barked at Elisabeth as she'd got moodily out of the car, "To ensure his son enjoys the lifetime's benefits of a robust name."
Elisabeth threw him a doubtful glance. "Robust?"
"It means sturdy."
Elisabeth knew what it meant; she just couldn't believe he'd said it. "My God" she thought woefully, "He thinks the boy is a table!"

But Jim was right; Elisabeth had no choice in the matter. She wouldn't understand the forms they had to sign so inevitably the final decision lay with him. Still, Elisabeth was determined not to swallow this particular battle's loss with her usual equanimity and had perched herself on the bench once they'd arrived at the town hall, refusing to show any interest in either the old building's elaborate décor or what Jim had haughtily described as the 'legitimisation of their son's identity'. With the baby on her lap, Elisabeth contemplated the stucco walls and marbled floor tiles stretching the length of the corridor; normally wide eyed at such grandeur, today she found her surroundings only reflected the pomposity of her husband. Jim hadn't called her over to sign the birth certificate yet and Elisabeth began to wonder if this was yet another part of the proceedings in which she was expendable.

"Obviously so" she muttered under her breath, watching him turn away from the registrar and walk towards her.

"All done. Let's go," he said, taking the child from her arms. "Well hello there Edward Arthur Sinclair!" he beamed at the swaddled infant, raising the bundle to eye level as if to examine it.

"Well, I've got the whole day off work. Thought I'd use some of my holiday time so we could all spend the day together."

It was obvious to Elisabeth that he expected some form of gratitude in her response. "Unbelievable" she seethed inwardly, "Absolutely unbelievable!" In silence, she took the baby from Jim's arms and strode defiantly through the cold, sombre foyer, out into the sunlight. As insipid and wintry as it was, its meagre warmth cheered her and by the time Jim had brought the car round and helped them both in, Elisabeth felt she was capable of looking at her husband with something less than fury.

Although Elisabeth was of no mind to allay the anger that brewed inside her, Jim was not of a conciliatory nature and the wordless feud would no doubt last as only long as she could stand it.

Suddenly Elisabeth felt exhausted. There were so many arguments left in her unvoiced, so many demands for respect and re-evaluation that she felt she deserved, that Elisabeth could not fathom a way to articulate them. All that remained was silence and it stood like a body of water between them, its tide tugging at them gently, pressing them in sometimes similar, sometimes separate directions. She wished that she could at least love him – and in that believe that there was some good to the life she had unwittingly chosen. It had begun to rain; before starting the engine, Jim reached over to ensure the small wicker basket in the back was secure. Elisabeth had pleaded for a new one to bring the baby home from hospital in. Instead Jim had appeared on the ward with yet another worn out hand-me-down from Margery. Now, as he grasped it, the softened weave shook violently beneath his hand.

"This little chap's going to need something sturdier. We'll have to buy a new one. I bet they're costly." He shifted in his seat and drummed his fingers on the steering wheel for a few seconds.

"Well, no time like the present I suppose. Where do we get one of those carrier things from?" he asked her matter-of-factly.

"BHS." she responded indifferently, feigning fascination for the gathering mist on the windscreen. Inwardly however, Elisabeth rejoiced; Jim had finally capitulated on something. Of course, he could afford to, he'd won the greater battle; "But all the same," she considered wryly, "I've won this one."

"What do you mean he won't let you christen him? Oh Beth, that's awful!"

Elisabeth didn't respond and Margot sat opposite her friend, watching her nervously wring out one of the napkins that had decorated the table. They were in the tea rooms on the fourth floor of Brown's, having ended their afternoon shopping excursion in the home-ware department two floors below.

"He must know what that means to you – and to your parents, surely?"

Elisabeth nodded glumly. "It's not a question of me though, is it? It's about the baby."

"My God, now you sound just like him! He said that didn't he?"

Elisabeth nodded again; Margot looked furious and she was beginning to wish she hadn't mentioned it. She didn't have the energy to rant as she felt she was expected to: Edward had been up all night and so she, of course, had been up with him.

Baptism was just one of the numerous things she and Jim had argued over regarding the baby's upbringing. True to form, from the minute they'd brought him home, Jim had claimed unwarranted authority in the little one's well being, criticizing Elisabeth's every action in caring for the child (whilst managing not to lift a finger to help her in the process). When she had bathed the boy she had been too hesitant; when she had dressed him, too rough. Thankfully, eight weeks on, her husband had grown bored of his role as self-appointed parenting mentor and had returned to his favourite place: the garage, to tinker under the bonnet of an old Aston martin that had stood rusting there for as long as Elisabeth could remember.

"You'll try to change his mind won't you?" Margot's insistent tone brought Elisabeth back to the present.

"I'll try." She knew the words meant little, their intent already laid waste; such blatant symbols of religion as christenings were anathema to Jim who remained staunch in his atheism.

"Money is the only god!" he had declared, arms held aloft in evangelical protest when she'd pressed him on the subject. The statement did not shock Elisabeth at all (although, as a good catholic, she knew it should have); upon those beliefs were built Jim's boundaries and each was cemented into place so as to cast their shadows on any intruding philosophies. These shadows were the walls within which man and wife existed, saturated with suspicion and unknowing of any other way.

Arriving home shortly before six, Elisabeth found Jim pacing the sitting room with Edward sobbing on his shoulder.

"You're late!" He barked. "Margery dropped him off half an hour ago. Little bugger hasn't stopped crying since." He tried to pass the baby to Elisabeth but she sidestepped him.

"Let me prepare his bath first, then I'll take him off your hands. Margery said she'd keep him 'til six. Was there a problem?"

Jim scowled in response; he was obviously in a foul temper.

"None - other than the fact that she has two other children to look after, Elisabeth."

"I'll be two minutes." She reassured him, backing out of the sitting room and into the darkened hall.

"You'd better," he answered brusquely. "I've been working all day - I shouldn't have to be doing this."

In the bathroom, Elisabeth ran a mixture of hot and cold water, half filling the hand basin. It was the first time she'd left the house without Edward and had hoped everything would go smoothly. She was annoyed that Margery had brought him back early, giving Jim yet another opportunity to berate her. Blatantly irritated at being left to the sole care of his son, he would find pleasure in filling the rest of the evening with acerbic remarks about the responsibilities of motherhood. Tired and tearful, Elisabeth sat on the edge of the bath, her fingers draped in the tepid water. She could hear Edward's cries and the rumbling baritone of her husband commanding the child to be quiet. Suddenly Edward's weeping escalated into a gut-wrenching howl. Elisabeth almost hurled herself down the stairs in an effort to reach them and threw open the sitting room door to see her husband sitting upright on the settee with the baby across his lap, naked but for a towelling nappy. The poor creature was on his belly, his thin arms flailing in desperation and his face as red as a cherry tomato.

"What the hell happened?" Elisabeth demanded, scooping the child up from Jim's knees.

"Don't make such a fuss Elisabeth." He regarded her calmly.

"Young children need to be disciplined occasionally."

Elisabeth's jaw dropped in disbelief. "You hit him?" she hissed.

"Spanked him, Elisabeth. After all, a father is responsible for his children's punishment."

Elisabeth gawped. "Punishment? For what?"

Jim got up from where he was sitting with an air of impatience.

"Being difficult of course. For keeping up that infernal whimpering and struggling as I tried to undress him. I swear he doesn't like me. By the way, have you seen my newspaper anywhere?"

Lost for words, Elisabeth carried Edward from the room, slamming the door behind her. Upstairs she laid her son on their bed and gently removed the nappy, rolling him onto his stomach to check his tiny bottom for markings.

The sight of a thick-fingered hand print bridging both cheeks caused a sob to catch in her throat. "How could he?" she gasped, tears spilling onto the bedclothes. Elisabeth lifted the still sniffling infant tentatively to her shoulder, avoiding as much as she could the inflamed pink flesh of his behind, and carried him to the bathroom where she bathed him gently, singing softly to him as she did so.

Soothed by the warm water and lullabies, Edward fell asleep almost as soon as his mother laid him in his cot. Elisabeth on the other hand was still distraught and incredulous – albeit tearless now. Instead her face was set in a stony expression, giving away no hint of the murderous thoughts tumbling around inside her. It was with that expression that she met her husband at the top of the stairs.

"I was coming up to say goodnight." he said amicably, letting her pass.

"Don't bother," she answered quietly, "He won't even know you're there."

"Oh well, another time then. How did the Christmas shopping go?"

The look on Jim's face was so nonchalant that Elisabeth wanted to slap him – to mark his cheek with finger prints the way he had his son's. Instead she brushed past him unspeaking, unwilling to absolve him with anything quite so trite and trivial as words.

Despite his good mood, Jim cursed under his breath as he struggled to unlock the back door with a baked ham wedged in the crook of one arm and several small packages balanced precariously in the other. He put the ham in the fridge and then carried the presents through to the sitting room to the corner where the tree stood. There were one or two boxes there already and a shapeless package Jim guessed to be woollens.

Each year, his sister Alma sent him either a knitted scarf or jumper which he rarely wore, preferring the more conventional Argyle sweaters he purchased on his annual spring visits to the menswear shops in Bradford when he felt obliged by the season's blossoming colours and fragrant rejuvenation to replenish the contents of his sock drawer.

Placing his packages with the rest, he took care not to knock the lower branches of the brightly lit tree. Elisabeth had decorated it a week earlier, draping silver tinsel artfully across each spiny arm and hooking glass baubles onto their tips. Pretending to be absorbed in his newspaper, Jim had watched her with fond amusement, enjoying the solemnity and concentration with which she'd wound the tiny fairy lights around the tree's verdant form, standing back to contemplate her work between minor adjustments. All the while, the baby gurgled, staring up at his mother from the rug on the floor with unwavering awe. This memory of them both made the house feel all the more quiet; he was not used to the place seeming so still.

Wondering if, exhausted from the late night feeds, Elisabeth was napping with Edward upstairs, Jim stuck his head around the sitting room door leading to the hallway. "Hello?" He called out and remained frozen for several seconds awaiting a response. There was none and the house, in spite of the glittering tree and warmth of the sitting room fire, seemed strangely derelict. Hanging his coat in the hall, Jim went upstairs and peered first into the baby's room and then their own; both were empty. "That is odd," he said aloud. "She can't be far" he thought, "She did leave the fire on after all." One day, Elisabeth's forgetfulness would have disastrous consequences.

Normally he would bristle at such careless but tonight he felt contented and full of Christmas cheer. It was their first Christmas together as a family and this year, rather than considering it one of the necessary tasks of the season, Jim had actually enjoyed picking out a present for Elisabeth, choosing bath salts and lotion from the ladies counter at Marks & Spencer's.

"Just what a busy new mum deserves!" The assistant had told him cheerfully as she'd wrapped them, noticing with quiet amusement the way his eyes darted back and forth self-consciously. Scanning the vast selection of bottles and jars on display, he had begun to feel overwhelmed. With so many colours and aromas to choose from, it was no wonder, he'd concluded, that women were indecisive. This rare flash of empathy had made Jim's head spin; he'd decided it was the pungent salts and had hurried from the store, keen to taste fresh air and return to the masculine familiarity of his shared office.

Once downstairs again, Jim made himself a cup of tea. At least the house was tidy, he observed, noting that that the kitchen surfaces were clear and the numerous piles of baby clothes and washing that had been strewn about the place that morning had all been put away. Unsure of when Elisabeth was returning and having seen no signs of a partially prepared meal on the stove, Jim decided to cut some ham and make a sandwich to eat whilst he watched TV. Elisabeth wouldn't be long; on such a cold night he knew she would not take Edward far. They were probably next-door but one, sitting at Margery's kitchen table, drinking tea. "After all" he thought, "There's the dinner to make and Edward needs a bath before putting to bed." Elisabeth was quite strict about that and Jim appreciated his wife's stringency in caring for his son. Maladroit in every other area of her life, it was obvious that she was making a special effort to keep on top of things where Edward was concerned. Jim switched on the television.

There was a football match on and although Jim preferred the faster paced sports of stock car racing and Formula One, it was good to watch a game every now and then, he reasoned. Elisabeth would soon be home; the boy would be tired and grouchy, the house once more awash with his tiny crocodile tears. Making himself comfortable on the settee with the cup of tea in his hand and the ham sandwich on his lap, he settled down to wait for them, reminding himself that it was good to have time alone.

As the taxi drove slowly, navigating the darkness and icy roads, what were once familiar streets with welcoming houses appeared to Elisabeth drab and foreboding, their pitched silhouettes looming towards her through the misty glass. She sat with her gaze fixed on the passing shapes and shadows, grateful for the driver's silence and the soft leather seats that acknowledged her aching frame with placating creaks and acquiescent cushions. There was the reassuring tang of tobacco in the air, a lingering perfume like that of a pipe. Her father smoked a pipe – or had done when she was a child; Elisabeth breathed the aroma in as if she were breathing in her father.

"This is the street love. What number?" the driver spoke quietly over his shoulder, not wanting to wake the sleeping child swathed in blankets on the woman's lap. The poor girl looked so tired, he thought, and almost too fragile to mother a kid.

When picking her up from the pleasant cul-de-sac in Baildon (which had held the rarefied air of young families and Christmas expectations; their unified excitement shining in the coloured lights that decorated every window) he had been ready to chat about the tediousness of family visits and cooking large dinners – or some such similar piffle with which passengers had filled his ears all day. But there had been a pleasant stoicism to the sad smile she had given him as he'd reached for her suitcase and put it in the trunk; a look that had wordlessly reassured him it would be a quiet journey. He liked to think of himself as a kind man, a caring man, a man who had been driving taxis for fourteen years and seen that expression a thousand times before - a man who knew well the value of comfortable silence. Her smile had asked nothing more of him than that; and it was an easy promise to honour.

Elisabeth saw, through the rain-splattered glass, the half rusted gate she knew guarded the path that led to her parents' front door.

"This is fine. I will only be two minutes, please wait here for me."

The voice that fell from her was timid, unable to decide between statement and question.

"No problem love. I'll be right here."

As she reached for the door handle he pondered for a second on whether or not she meant to leave the little one, forcing him to endure five minutes of startled tears should the child miss her. Hands still on the wheel, he watched patiently in the rear view mirror as the teenager lifted the bundle to her shoulder and expertly manoeuvred them both as one out of the car - and then reached for his pipe, scolding himself for having entertained such a selfish notion.

The air was still but brittle, biting at her cheeks as she walked the ten yards from the taxi towards the house. Elisabeth clutched Edward closer to her chest and swung open the gate, knowing that its perennial groan would bring one or the other of her parents to the window. A curtain twitched; it was her father, his soft face folding into a smile at the sight of her. As she reached the front step he was opening the door, mumbling sounds of surprise and pleasure.

"You should have said! Your mother is visiting with Mrs Wilson. We would have made tea." He reached for her as he said this, taking her arm and ushering her inside. Elisabeth stepped back, gently breaking his grasp.

"Dad, I can't stay."

Confused, her father glanced behind her, searching the poorly lit street for the figure her husband. "Is he waiting in the car?"

"No Dad, Jim isn't here. I caught a taxi." Elisabeth felt her eyes begin to burn and swell with tears. "I've left him Dad."

The words had sat on Elisabeth's lips for weeks and she had practised them under her breath whilst she'd dusted and cleaned and picked out a Turkey for Christmas. She had expected disapproval, not angry like her mother's, but a quiet disappointment that she would have to battle or apologise for; here on the doorstep of her childhood home, Elisabeth had not the heart for either.

As her father reached out to her, silently taking daughter and grandchild into his arms, Elisabeth bled all her tears with a sigh and whispered "Thank you".
"Its Christmas eve Elisabeth." he responded. "Stay here with us."
"I can't. This is the first place he'll come. I need some time."
"But time for what?"
"Just time - time to think I suppose."
With great pride, Henry William Robinson kissed his youngest, most precious child on the crown of her satin blonde head. He feared for her, as he did all his children, but this little one had given away so much of herself so young that all he could hope for was that there was enough left to start again. As a parent, he knew that Beth had merely crossed the border from childhood to adult like any other young woman – but he had no doubt that the poor girl had paid more dearly for it than most.
"Will you let your mother and I know where you are?"
"Of course I will – as soon as I'm settled. I'm staying with Margot until Boxing Day and then, well, we'll see." She didn't know what to tell him. Jim would come looking for her and she could not bear to think of her father lying for her, sharing her deceit. She envisaged the stand-down between father and son in law and the shadow it cast upon both men's characters, one man's demands sparring with the other's denials; Elisabeth did not wish this on either of them.
Her father walked with her back to the taxi, carrying Edward, and waited until Elisabeth was comfortably sat before placing his grandchild tenderly on her lap. He reached in to brush away a strand of hair from her forehead. "Take care of yourself Elisabeth. And this little lad here." he said, stoking a thick, wizened finger across the baby's cheek. The infant stirred in his mother's arms.
"I will. Merry Christmas Dad."
"Merry Christmas Elisabeth."
The taxi's engine started. The old man, crooked with the cold in his thin cardigan and carpet slippers, held the door open just a few seconds longer to steal one last look at his child and grandchild. He knew it might be some while before he saw them again.

Hotel Room

He talks; I sit and listen, nodding my head in continuous acknowledgement. After a while my head grows dizzy and I change to long, comprehending smiles. The sun left us about an hour ago. Now leaden clouds gather, tumescent with rain, forming a dull grey blanket that will sooner or later suffocate me. Two staccato voices move urgently along the passage: another injustice taking place somewhere. We stop for a second to listen and then eye one another in supposed superior understanding of the world we have trapped outside that door; the stained wooden door leading to the stained sodden corridor of this dead-end avenue hotel room we have chosen for the afternoon.

"Aren't we wicked?" he croons, dripping affectation, and stretches those solid, deeply tanned limbs that only a half hour ago had pinned me to the bed.

"Shame it's a one-off really." he laughs, searching my face for disappointment. He will find none. My gaze drifts over his head to the window and a thousand tiny explosions as each droplet throws itself against the glass. I feel like doing the same. Instead I think about the man I love. My last words to him were "Take the fruitcake with you." I wonder if he will ever forgive me that. I know that he would never forgive me this.

"Shall we leave now?" he smiles, rising. My mind wanders resentfully back towards my body.

"And my point of view?" I ask sweetly.

"Oh that." he coos, his smug smile as saccharin as mine. "I think I covered everything. Is there anything else?" His lazy nonchalant shrug indicating that the question is rhetorical. As expected of me, I say nothing. I have made myself worthless and deserve nothing more. As I presume the pills will, words sit bitterly on my tongue and I resist the urge to spit them out.

Satisfied, he leaves. I stay, "Just a little longer." I tell myself, to inhale the odour with which our shallow union has imbued the room. There are no fond goodbyes and as the lock clicks, my body slumps further in to the chair, my spirit tumbling deeper in to that huge physical wasteland that is our sex.

Evensong

They were nearly out of gin – just enough left for a decent double. Why hadn't he thought of that when nipping out for the tonic? Still, Bruce smiled; there was enough, that's all that mattered. He washed the lemon before slicing it. God knows what they coat these things in, he thought as he ran it under the tap; rubbing his thumb across its stippled, yellow skin.

From the bush beneath the kitchen window, the whirr of cicadas tuning their wings for evensong reminded him he had little time. He returned from the dining room with a small silver platter and on it, quickly arranged the glass into which he had poured the gin, a small bottle of tonic water and a saucer decorated with several slices of the freshly cut lemon. The clock began to chime. Bruce stood passively, waiting until it had struck six times before scooping up the house keys and pushing them into his back pocket. As his hand reached for the tray, Bruce paused and frowned, his eyes studying its contents. What he needed now was a napkin.

It was still very warm outside and he felt the sun on his face the second he stepped down from the veranda. What a perfect evening, he mused, contemplating the voluminous frangipani bushes that lined the garden's entrance, their sweet, delicate scent soothing the tensions of what had been a hot summer's day. Across the street, his neighbour, Jan, wearing a chain mail of soapsuds and armed with a sponge, was engaged in battle with the garden hose. Chrissie, his wife, stood on the front steps laughing raucously at her husband as he tried to wash his car, delighted by his inability to manoeuvre himself between the bucket behind him and the violent jet of water from the unruly pipe. Amidst the struggle, it was Jan who first noticed the solid figure in shorts and T-shirt emerge from the garden opposite; one hand at his brow in a careless salute, shading his face from the sun, the other balancing a cloth covered tray, high at his shoulder, like a waiter would.

Jan called out to him. "Hello Bruce!"

Chrissie simply cocked her head and waved.

"Good evening all" Bruce responded, slowing his pace just a little.

The question on their lips was obvious and quickly spread, in the form of a bemused look, to their faces. He knew they would not ask, but would say "There goes Bruce," to each other once he had passed, their eyebrows cocked in mutual understanding. Bruce was not bothered by it. He was in good humour that day and happy for them to share with him, the absurdity of the scene. Jan and Chrissie were good people. He knew they liked him; and that they were fond, even, of his singular ways and frivolous exploits. Others were crueller and keen to judge: usually those closest to him, friends and relatives who felt that they had earned through familiarity their right to criticise. Although well meant, it was still hurtful. How had he so frustrated them with his harmless antics? And why was it, he wondered, that such simple actions or spontaneous gestures could be seen as superficial and their bearer, insincere? There were sad moments when he felt himself, like his humour, to have been grossly misjudged. In these moments his thoughts would fracture and he'd scramble amongst them (like a child hunts pebbles on a beach) handpicking perspectives with which to appease himself. When there were none to be found, he would turn to his books and find a quiet place - away from life's light and noise, where he could sit and seek refuge in other, invented worlds.

Not today however. Today he had enjoyed the sun peeking through the living room windows as he'd vacuumed, marvelling at the rods of light it cast across the carpet and giggling as he'd tried to suck them up. Today he'd left his books untouched and gone instead to the beach and walked along the shore, tracing its curve from one cliff face to the other. For almost an hour he'd sat on the sand and watched the surfers paddle about on their boards, waiting patiently for the next opportunity to pitch their skill against the waves. It was impressive, the number of dumps they were willing to take in order to hitch that one perfect ride into shore. Bruce watched in wonderment as again and again, they tumbled onto the sand. He was amazed at how these svelte creatures, undaunted by the angry buffeting they'd just received, could, with relish, press their bodies back in to the foaming water and re-mount their boards without any question of danger or doubt. You never know, Bruce had thought, perhaps they did. But he liked to think they didn't: the surfers', if not dogged, then naïve persistence was to Bruce, a triumph of spirit.

    Walking home from the beach that day, encouraged by the revelation, he had searched his own life for such triumphs and was relieved and thankful to have found some. Not all were feats of strength or skill; some were moments of kindness or compassion - measures of character Bruce felt to be equally honourable and no less profound. He'd spent his life making people laugh (or trying to), could it have been better spent, nobler or more profound than that?

    Refreshed and self-satisfied, he returned home that afternoon in a very pleasant state of mind; so pleasant in fact that he felt that he should act upon it, show some appreciation for the gifts the day had given him.

The street was quiet, so rather than negotiate the clefts and crevices of the poorly maintained pavement, Bruce strolled the length of the road, ignoring the heat of the tarmac seeping through his sandals. He could feel the prickles of sweat beneath his T-shirt dampening the hair on his chest, and hoped it wouldn't soak through before he'd reached the bus stop.

    Although it was only at the end of the road, the buses from the city stopped on the other side so he'd have to cross over. Waiting for the lights to change, he felt curiously invisible amongst the throng of homebound commuters. It was the end of another long day and the sun had begun to wane. People wanted to get home to who or whatever it was that was waiting for them. Some, he imagined, would change hurriedly and head down to the beach pool for a swim or evening surf. Others would be cataloguing in their heads, the small things left to purchase in order to make dinner. Bruce could always recognise these; their stride would narrow as they passed the entrance to Franklins and he would watch them struggle with the image of their sore, heavy feet having to traipse up and down trolley filled aisles only to find themselves at the end of a stagnant queue, clutching no more than one or two items. The question "Is it worth it?" was always on their faces. Of course it was likely most had sat snugly behind partitions, clucking to one another like caged hens all day, but others, he knew, had walked several miles between desks and photocopiers – or back and forth in their two-inch heels, across the highly polished floors of Sydney's large department stores. He thought again of his wife and his heart reached out towards her. It was her image he saw stepping timidly across those vast, slippery floors.

She would be home soon, asking Bruce about his day, knowing it had been an easy one. He vowed to weave a tale from it, with which to make her smile; sharing it with her, the only way he could.

Bruce reached the bus stop just in time to see the 190 express from Wynyard turn left, out of Newport loop and back on to the main highway where it merged with the traffic and began to descend the hill towards him. Dusk's opal light made it impossible to distinguish anything beyond the windscreen until the bus had hissed to a standstill in front of him. It was then that he spotted her. She was sat by the window, distracted in her impatience at the scores of people in front of her, all queuing to get off. He knew she would be tired and frustrated at being forced once more into acquiescence by the other passengers, seeing it as yet another reminder of how she spent her days.

Bruce knew how much Hilary hated her job. She worked as an assistant manager in a woman's retailers in one of Pitt Street's many arcades. He'd found it difficult to get work recently and they'd both become very stressed by the mounting bills and constant demands of their two teenage children. As a result, there had been many arguments – mainly about money, though both knew that wasn't the cause. It was the reversal of familial roles neither could come to terms with. His wife's entrapment as the breadwinner in a role that was far beneath her had jarred both Bruce's self esteem and hers; and though they had talked it through many times and knew their only enemy was circumstance, alone in their thoughts, each felt strangely subjugated by the other.

Still poised with the tray at his shoulder, Bruce realised it was possible that she wouldn't notice him until the sea of bodies had dispersed. That would be awkward; dodging elbows and brief cases with a string of mumbled apologies. Luckily, as she rose from her seat she turned – probably to check she'd not forgotten anything – and saw him, stood casually grinning at her from the pavement. She noticed the napkin and platter immediately. Bruce thought he saw her cheeks redden and grinned more broadly.

"What on earth are you doing?" she mouthed through the glass.

He considered his grin a response. Shaking her head, Hilary quickly gathered her things and urged her way past those that were dithering. His eyes followed her all the way down the aisle. Others about her had noticed too, his gaze guiding them to her face. Several women smiled knowingly, glancing over their shoulders at her as if they had been in on the conspiracy the whole time. Softened by their wistful looks, the frown on Hilary's face had faded and now she stood, waiting to disembark, wearing a mischievous smile of her own. Finally she reached the steps.

"Bruce!" she laughed, her arms spread in question of him.

He bowed as deeply as he dare and with a flourish, whipped the napkin from its platter. "Madame. Your gin and tonic."

Seeing the glass, the bottle, the slices of lemon fanned out upon the saucer - all held aloft by her daft, beautiful husband; Hilary laughed with astonishment and then pursed her lips in mock severity.

"Well then Bruce, I suppose you should pour it before it gets warm!"

Bruce tipped his head once more; delighted she'd caught the thread of the joke. "Yes ma'am – lemon?"

"Well of course Bruce!"

They drank the gin and tonic together, ambling up the street and giggling at the unlikely prospect of an evening home alone. Sat on the steps, inhaling the garden flowers' sweet incense and sucking the last of the juice from the lemon, Hilary turned sombrely to Bruce and thanked him.

"Why?" he asked

"For stealing the day and saving the night."

"That's a funny response!"

"Yes" she shrugged "True though".

Bruce said nothing. He knew exactly what she meant. In her pale, green eyes, he saw more than love and gratitude. Bruce saw the anguish and frustrations of her day - every tedious hour that had clung to her limbs and rounded her shoulders, fade and then vanish, leaving only his reflection. It awed him that he was capable of making that happen. 'A triumph of spirit!' he laughed inwardly.

Hilary threw a piece of rind in his direction. "What are you smirking at!" she demanded.

He leant over and kissed her on the mouth. Her lips were soft and tasted of lemons. "I've thought about you all day".

"Argued with me, you mean!" she scoffed.

"Well…yes"

"What were we debating?"

"Everything!" he exclaimed, "And I won."

Hilary eyed him slyly, "You always do when I'm not there."

"Yes," he said, his body beginning to stir beneath her gaze, "But it's never as much fun."

Just a Rose

As winter's frost thawed more and more to dew and spring's young sun awoke from his sleep amongst the clouds, far below in a long lost or hidden garden stood a rose bush. Seduced by the unfamiliar sensation of warmth's first embrace, the frail young bush had given birth to a single bud, its tiny form pink and perfect. Around the bush lay a verdant carpet of grass and small flowers like bright satin stitches, threading themselves through one another so as to embroider the unkempt garden with a delicate pattern of gold, blue, red and lilac. As the days grew warmer and the sun more potent, butterflies would visit, dancing like fairies from stem to stem until each found their place amongst the clustered petals. There they would rest awhile, swaying in unison with the blossoms beneath a milky cerulean sky. The lonely bud, still wrapped inside her guardian's cloak, prayed patiently for the tight green fist to slacken so that she may bask in the light like the others. The more she pressed against her cell, the tighter it pinched her tumescent form. Frustrated and helpless, she waited.

Dawn appeared and dusk fell time and time again. The young sun, gaining in strength each day, shone with renewed vigour upon the garden. Stretching their limbs with a yawn, the trees unfurled their leaves and more blossoms burst their pods in garish triumph. Still the rose bush held tight and the bud began to swell, her delicate pink frills stealthily prising the rim of her guardian's armour. Honeybees came - lured by the flowers, who'd tossed their scents to the wind and now lay languorously in the heat, spreading themselves generously for their visitors to feed upon. Laden with berries, the garden had become a larder of sweet and succulent provisions and began to rustle and hum with the movement of small creatures. Soon a family of squirrels ventured in to spend their days playing and making love amongst the branches of the gnarled and shady oaks that formed the garden's boundary.

Weeks passed and for all of summer's persuasion, the possessive bush would not release its offspring and gradually the young bud's stem - parched by heat and the fervent struggle to blossom - began to lean a little under her weight. Dawn's dew and dusk's glow, try all they might, could not assist the buds escape nor persuade her captor to unlock its chamber even momentarily so that she might stretch free of it. The air grew cold and discouraging. Exhausted in her attempt at freedom, the young rose quietly resigned herself to peering out from beneath the shroud, her colour fading quickly as the soft laced frills faltered, their rusted trim shrivelled as if singed.

It wasn't long before the rains came and with them autumn winds that snatched the bronzed and ochre leaves from their weather-beaten hosts to darn a rustic quilt across the sleepy garden. Lulled by the season's effort, the dull and ageing sun once again grew pallid and began to pass his short-lived days safely tucked within the clouds that had gathered bulk to cradle him.

Flaccid in death, the bud now swung back and forth like a bell, its silent toll signalling the autumn's end. Storms soon brewed the clouds to broth and pierced the skies with angry bolts, whose deep bass notes coursed the earth and tore the trees from their roots. The stubborn bush relaxed its fist and let its rotting hostage fall to earth.

The severed head quickly grew putrid as it merged with the mud at the base of its mother. As valiant as she had been in her fight for life, despite such glorious potential, still the newborn bud, for all her struggle, had remained (like the many who came and went before her) insubstantial and unseen. Just another rose that failed to blossom.

Lady on a Train

The guard's whistle shrilled one last time and the train slid grudgingly forward. Two stooped figures clutching one another on the platform faded until I could no longer see them. Finally the entire station out of view, I allowed one indulgent sigh and let the image of my parents slip comfortably away. Pouring myself into the first available seat, I closed my eyes and immediately felt the weight of consciousness sinking within me, After only a few seconds, it had anchored itself firmly, most joyously in sleep.

"You don't approve of the woman, my dear?" The voice, like chalk upon a blackboard, dragged me cruelly from my unconscious state.

A similarly grating voice replied. "It's not a matter of don't approve, Helena, I just don't think she makes a very convincing widow."

Opening one resentful eye, I gave an involuntary start; sitting across from me were two middle-aged women, one thin, one fat – and both undeniably frumpish. The larger woman reached into a crocheted bag and pulled out a bundle of knitting.

"Frankly, I don't believe a woman like that, about to inherit an estate from her husband, could possibly be grieving."

"I suppose not." Her companion replied doubtfully.

"I mean, look at that, not even wearing black – red dress indeed! Disgraceful" The woman raised a fat hand and gestured to towards an area behind me. Aware that they would realise I had been listening, I thought it too obvious to turn and look. Typical of my curious nature, by the time the conversation had drifted on to another, more normal topic, I was so determined to sneak a glance at this 'scarlet widow' that I moved away under the pretence of going to the bathroom.

Her head was to the window and, wanting to see her face, I mustered up a rather pathetic cough. She glanced my way and as she did, I felt my heart skip a beat. It was the loveliest face I'd ever seen: a canopy of thick black lashes shading pale green eyes; skin as smooth as buttermilk, so translucent I could see her cheek-bones. Wow! I thought. That's what a murderess looks like?

Being one of the last to arrive at the dining car, I found myself placed next to the two middle-aged women who were deep in conversation with an elderly gentleman and a woman I deduced to be his wife. I wasn't taking much notice; all I could think about was the young widow who'd just entered. The fat woman's companion had obviously noticed her too, as she turned to her friend and exclaimed "Ooh Mary, Look!" The fat woman raised a disapproving eyebrow and proceeded to tell the doctor and his wife about the mysterious lady in red.

"You think there's foul play?" The doctor's wife demanded, spirited at the prospect of gossip.

"You think she planned it, don't you Mary?" the thin woman whispered. Mary's bosom began to swell with importance. "It's not a matter of *think* Helena. Mrs Harding and I, that's her name by the way, have the same hairdresser."

The doctor looked doubtful, "You don't think its just talk?"

"Certainly not!" She huffed. "She tells the hairdresser everything and the hairdresser tells me!"

The doctor's wife turned on me. "What do you think?"

"I, I don't know." I stammered, shocked at my sudden inclusion into the conversation. "I don't know her."

"Just as well." The fat lady scowled. "Not the kind of company to keep!"

"Do you really think she did it?" I asked.

"There's an awful lot of money involved, four million to be precise."

This brought an appreciative whistle from the doctor, inspiring the woman to go further. "He was an old man as well, not a day under sixty-five!"

I had to admit, it sounded strange. Four million dollars is a lot of money, I thought, people have killed for less. Suddenly we were in complete darkness.

"Typical!" The doctor growled. "As soon as it gets the dark the generator goes. It'll be doing it all night, just you watch!"

He was right; by the end of dinner we found ourselves in darkness not less than fifteen times. I didn't mind it personally, it appealed to my sense of adventure. There's something about it that makes one raise one's voice; the peculiar assumption that if they can't see you, they can't hear you either. We'd almost exhausted the subject of the enigmatic Mrs Harding when it dawned on me just how far our voices may have carried. I looked around only to see her storming from the car. Consumed by guilt, I swung round to face my dinner companions and was incredulous to find them completely unperturbed. Suddenly I hated them, hated what they'd said, and most of all hated myself for listening to them. Jason, I thought as I left the table, you're a real jerk!

I found her in one of the compartments, tucked away in the corner. Not knowing what to do, I just stood there, listening to her cry with her head between hands. It seemed minutes before she finally lifted her face to look at me. Those eyes that had so entranced me earlier were bloodshot and swollen; her skin had flushed pink and there were tearstains across her cheek.

"I am so sorry." I stuttered. Seeing that delicate face contorted in misery, I didn't know what to say. She looked so beautiful that like an idiot I told her so.

"Don't. DON'T!" She cried, covering her head with her arms.

"That's all they see - a pretty girl who married a rich old man."

Letting her arms drop into her lap, she lifted her head until her gaze met mine. "If once, just once, they'd looked hard enough, they'd see that I loved him!"

Saddened and humiliated, I returned to my seat. I sat and watched, waiting for her. Fifteen minutes later I still hadn't seen her. I must have fallen asleep, for the first thing I remember was being thrown from my seat by some invisible source. It was dark but I could hear the voices of the other passengers raised in panic. A conductor was racing past so I reached out an arm and grabbed him. "What is it?" I demanded. "Why have we stopped? Is it the generator?"

"Wish it was" the conductor shook his head sadly. "Some woman's thrown herself off the train."

The Smell of Rain

The relief of finishing work early vanished the second Sarah stepped out of the lift and into reception. Instead of the soft grey tones of dusk she had hoped for, beyond the foyer's glass façade lay in wait a moody darkness. "Oh please" she thought "Please don't let it be raining." She'd left her brolly (or more accurately, her boyfriend's brolly) in the café where she'd met Sally at lunchtime. Mark wouldn't be pleased; she'd been banned from borrowing it. Sarah wasn't very good at looking after umbrellas – or any other accessory for that matter. Recognising this absent-mindedness as an inherent part of her nature, Sarah had become almost philosophical about the number of scarves, hats and gloves she had surrendered to the maw of London's transport system. It pleased her somehow to think that the abandoned woollies might have been adopted by other, more worthy commuters who, after carrying their newfound treasures home, would wash them tenderly by hand to erase the scent of her perfume and then wear them and love them – and not treat them carelessly, as Sarah had done. Mark was a little more pragmatic on the subject. Sarah knew she was in for a lecture and, with it being so close, no doubt Christmas would be mentioned.

This would be their fifth year living together. Each year, a week before Christmas, Mark would appear at the door, dragging behind him a fir tree. Great ceremony would be made of its dressing – which was something Mark always insisted upon doing alone. Sarah would sit on the couch and watch, sipping a glass of wine and marvelling at the amount of pride and care he took in dressing its spiny limbs with baubles and ribbons. He looked so childishly content, rifling through the 'occasions box' as he called it, in search of paper trinkets. The box, which Mark kept on the top shelf of the airing cupboard, was a treasure trove of shiny decorations. Not only Christmas decorations but also balloons, children's 'Happy Birthday' banners and even some crepe paper snowflakes that concertinaed into a string of glorious multi-coloured lanterns. Sarah had no idea where all these things had come from - she'd never seen him buy any of it. Mark had something of the magpie in him and almost every cupboard in the flat housed at least one box of 'useful things' that, contrary to the felt tip exclamations scrawled across each one, were rarely, if ever, actually used.

Beneath the Christmas tree so lovingly adorned, every year - without fail, amongst the tidy pile of offerings from Mark would be a carefully wrapped glove and scarf set from Marks & Spencer's. Always the same style, he would quiz her on his choice of size and colour, vowing never to buy her such things ever again should she lose them this time.

"Good!" Sarah often retorted light-heartedly, "If you bought me something more interesting, I'd probably keep hold it of longer!"

Mark would laugh at this, knowing it not to be true and then launch with a serious voice into one of his diatribes. "Cherishing something doesn't guarantee you against its loss, Sarah" and so on. Mark was full of pithy statements like those, witty aphorisms with which he painted himself as the epitome of common sense.

And perhaps he was right to do so. He was indeed the epitome of common sense as far as she was concerned. Mark was the most sensible man Sarah had ever met and of course she loved him dearly for it - most of the time. What nagged at Sarah was the worrying sensation of boredom. Sarah's inability to define and therefore identify the feeling bothered her greatly. Was Mark bored? Or was it that Mark bored her? On reflection, their life had become a little predictable and most weekends were spent *in* rather than *out*, but had they changed that much, she wondered. Their combined sense of humour as sharp as ever, she and Mark still laughed at each other's antics and daft observations. They argued sometimes of course, mainly about money - or Sarah's carelessness if Mark was feeling moody. It was one of his favourite niggles, having the distinct advantage over her on that subject. Sarah was careless and she knew it. She also knew that Mark loved her all the more for it. He saw in it an element of naivety that he said, lent her a girlish charm. Not as naive as she appeared, Sarah knew that it was in fact the assumed helplessness with which he associated her 'girlish charm' that had drawn him to her in the first place. Mark longed to play the carer - and Sarah was the perfect subject. With their futures unfurling just as she and Mark had planned, what was it that Sarah wanted to change?

She peered out from beneath the portico, planning her escape route through the quieter streets of London Bridge. The other option was to catch a bus along Southwark Bridge Road, but then they were always so crowded at this time of day. It wasn't unusual for two to fly past together, both drivers hell bent on ignoring the ten pairs of arms flapping ferociously at them from the bus stop. Better to get wet walking than waiting, she decided. Staring dolefully down at her feet, Sarah wished she'd worn sturdier shoes. Open toe heels, what on earth was she thinking? Union Street was her best bet. Criss-crossed by railway lines, it at least offered several bridges under which she could take cover should the downpour get worse. Again, she thought about Mark's brolly. "Why, oh why, oh why" she muttered aloud and stepped gingerly out into the rain. The building's security guard, who had been sneaking the last of an earlier rolled cigarette in the shadows behind her, came forward to the top of the steps and flicked the butt out beyond the pavement and into the gutter with a practiced dexterity. He watched Sarah cross the busy road, pre-occupied with dodging puddles, his gaze willing her safely through the traffic as she leapt gracefully into the path of one car after another. A faint smile penetrated his worn, ruddy face. "Mad as a hatter!" he muttered, and slid back into the shadows of the portico to roll another cigarette.

Half drenched already, Sarah hesitated at the corner of Great Suffolk Street, wondering whether to nip across to The Cut for a pack of cigarettes or make her way straight home in the hope that the half-packet she'd stashed with the grass in her sock drawer was still there. There was no reason why it shouldn't be, Mark rarely smoked anymore. He allowed himself the odd one at parties when he'd drunk too much; but other than that, he never touched them.

"It's a matter of keeping the habit in its place." he'd told her the night before, when she had lit up after dinner.

"I hardly smoke a lot" Sarah had replied haughtily, miffed at his spoon-feeding her guilt the second she did something he disapproved of. "Anyway, you hypocrite, you smoked thirty a day when I met you!"

"Ah but what's relevant is, do I smoke them now?"

There it was, another of Mark's infuriating little retorts. Sarah had not been in the mood to be patronised. "God forbid I might do anything even remotely dangerous! Really, Mark, could you possibly make life any duller? It's bad enough as it is!"

She had watched the remark hit him square in the chest and felt him recoil. His lower jaw pushed fractionally forward, Mark had got up from the table, his pasta unfinished.

"Well, if by trying so hard to make our lives easier, I've made them duller – I'm sorry for that"

Sarah had caught sight of the defeated expression on his face as he'd turned away. Realising too late that he hadn't deserved her outburst and that her words had not only been cruel but untrue, Sarah had said nothing as Mark took his dishes to the sink and left the room.

Of course, she had felt horrid about it and said so to Sally at lunch. "I don't really know what I expected" she moaned, a little childishly, "But this isn't it!"

Sally just smiled and tugged a serviette from its dispenser.

"I do love him!" Sarah added, hastily.

"Well that I know!" her friend responded, rolling her eyes.

"That's not really the issue, is it?"

Sarah knew what was coming. They'd had this conversation before.

Sally wiped her mouth and threw down the napkin. "You need a fling, or a flirtation, or… something!"

"I know it's difficult to grasp, but I don't do that Sally". She said it slowly, enunciating each word.

Sally raised an eyebrow, "Ouch!"

Suddenly Sarah melted, "Oh Sal, I'm sorry, I just didn't think".

Sally had only recently, been dumped by a man that she had dearly loved; a kind, considerate, handsome man who, unfortunately, just happened to have a wife.

"Ah, it's okay, I'll live." As she said this, Sally flicked both wrists, flashing her palms in that inimitable Jewish fashion.

Sal, Sarah noted, was turning into her mother. She contemplated telling her then thought better of it. As sweet as her mother was, Sarah knew Sally wouldn't take it as a compliment. Instead she sat quietly, listening to her friend gripe over the lack of fresh male talent in her building.

"We're in the heart of the business sector for God's sake! I mean, I work in a solicitor's god damn it - there should be swarthy men in suits lurking around every air-conditioned corner!" Sally took a swig from her Highland spring, smacking her lips as if it were whisky. "My life was supposed to be LA Law! That's how I'd planned it! Instead it's coagulated into one long episode of, of…"

Sarah saw Sally struggle. "Ally McBeal?"

"Yes! Yes! That's it! Ally bloody McBeal!" Sally was fit to bust now and on a roll.

"Bloody vicious, glamorous women with their sleek suits and silly dresses with Princess Di lapels - bloody loads of them, scratching at the office doors and partitions of the few eligible samples of male species who –" Sally stopped to suck in air, "aren't gay, married – to either a wife or their mates – cruel, spiteful or completely un-sexy. In fact the only eligible men in Ally McBeal were nerds! Isn't that weird? It's just occurred to me! We're being programmed to fall in love with nerds!"

Sal seemed satisfied that she'd made her point and took another long draught of water with a flourish of triumph. Suddenly her eyebrows shot up and she leaned forward.

"Speaking of swarthy men. Don't tell me you haven't noticed that Mr Gorgeous over there has been checking you out since we sat down."

Sally had, but had done her best to ignore him, which was difficult; the man was indeed gorgeous. Slimly built, with that devastating combination of wavy black hair and blue eyes, his were looks that were guaranteed to make a girl wistful. He'd entered wearing a raincoat that was now resting over the back of the chair beside him. She'd noticed because it was similar to Marks, a pale olive with tartan lining - but obviously much more expensive. At that moment, he turned to catch her looking at him and flashed her a smile. Sarah noticed that his teeth were white and even. Sally almost squealed. "Did you see that? Oh wow! You are so in!"

Sarah shot Sally a dangerous look, "Yes Sal, I am 'so in' – so in a relationship!"

Sally aimed one back, "Really madam, you are no fun at all, no wonder you're boring – oops sorry did I say that? I mean bored."

Sarah really hadn't expected that. "Ouch" she yelped, genuinely hurt.

Sally laughed and stuffed the last of a blueberry muffin into her mouth. "Aha, one all!" she cried, spitting crumbs.

That afternoon, Sarah had found herself at a loose end and seizing the moment, had nipped out of the office for coffee. They had a little kitchen on her floor which housed one of those American glass pot percolators but Sarah had a fondness for lattes and escaped the office in search of them whenever she could; she found them comforting, particularly on rainy days, and felt that the milk somehow nullified the caffeine (oh how Mark had laughed at that one). There was a Coffee Republic on the corner but the café where she'd had lunch with Sally was only one street away and made great takeaway coffees. Sarah had decided to steal a little of the remaining daylight and take a stroll.

As she had walked, she had become aware of the constant chorus of honks, hoots and the hiss of pistons around her. The traffic had already begun to congest (it seemed to start earlier in winter, or maybe it was just that there were more cars). Sarah had wondered where they all went. Where exactly, she had thought, did all those sales reps and executives, those flashy city boys and media girls who drove the two miles in from the cool parts of Hackney in their fuel guzzling jags and over polished minis, hide their prizes 'til home time? There must be a maze of secreted car parks, she decided, ramps leading into the foundations of buildings, twisting and winding through the clay and concrete, leading to vast, dimly lit caverns, each neatly divided by a grid of white lines.

Sarah had reached the café, still pondering the busy world beneath her feet when, just inside the door, she had found herself confronted by the man in the raincoat she'd seen earlier. He was holding a Styrofoam cup and was obviously as surprised to see her, as she was, him. He'd smiled, a little flustered, uncertain smile that was therefore even more seductive than the one he'd served her at lunch. "We keep running into each other. This is the second time, I wonder where the third will be?"

"Considering our track record, here – probably" she'd muttered, pointing to the cup he was holding, "I'm here for one of those."

He had cocked his head very slightly to one side, giving Sarah the impression she'd said something far more mysterious.

"Seems we share the same habits."

Sarah had felt the colour rise to her cheeks and had desperately wished it away. Gallantly the man had not pushed the conversation further but smiled once again, more knowingly this time, and with just a nod of his head, had left.

Sarah had stood for a moment in the centre of the cafe, feeling disorientated. Had he come on to her? Or was that just banter, the type that men and women often engage in? She'd decided it was just banter (therefore freeing her from any guilty feelings of misconduct) and went to the counter to order her latte. Walking back to the office, Sarah had turned the conversation over and over in her head. She tried not to, but every time she pushed him to one side, he would re-appear on the other. Sarah knew the antidote for that one, a vaccination of sense and sensibility to immunise her from sexy, sordid thoughts. She knew that what she needed was an injection of Mark - safe, secure, loveable Mark. Keeping one eye on the pavement, with its numerous fault lines and fissures, Sarah had pulled her mobile out of her handbag and sent him a text message: a short, cryptic message, reminding him of their first 'consummated' encounter on the roof of a council block in Vauxhall, many years before.

By the time she reached the office, there had still been no response. "Surely he must remember," she'd thought, trying hard not to feel dismal about it, "Surely he must."

When they'd first met at the London School of Economics, both being from small agricultural towns (hers in the north, his in the south), Mark had been as eager as she to explore the bustling delights of the city. Night after night they had hit the pubs and clubs of central London, crawling home at dawn across Waterloo Bridge, their first lecture of the day often starting just a few hours later. But by their second semester there, Sarah had immersed herself wholeheartedly in the cultural void of students' bars and house parties and it had taken Mark, who had grown bored of nursing her through the crippling hangovers, months of nagging to guide Sarah back towards her studies. Eventually she had capitulated and with Mark's support, Sarah had gone on to do well in her law degree and now had a good job with one of London's more prominent solicitors' offices. Mark, who ironically dropped out of law in his third year to study graphic design, had begun building his own business from home. Always the realist, Mark's dreams for the future consisted of a steady income from a reliable business that would one day pay the mortgage on a tidy little house and support them both when Sarah was ready to have children. Needless to say, her parents loved him.

It was dark now. Without warning, the sky split open and the decision was made for her; Sarah abandoned all interest in cigarettes and dashed for the nearest railway bridge, fifty yards to her right. She was not at all fond of the numerous railway arches that shaped the streets of London Bridge. In the premature darkness of winter afternoons, their unnerving gloom made her uneasy. Now, however, its shelter from the rain made the low arch seem hospitable and she sunk gratefully into its depth. It took a minute or two for Sarah to realise that she was not alone. For a moment, she could see no one but sensed the presence of another person. Trying not to panic, she peered into the darkness. As her eyes re-adjusted to the lack of light, so the figure became obvious. She recognised the pale olive raincoat immediately.

"Funny place to meet" he said, his voice low and even.

"Yes" Sarah half whispered, "It is." She was surprised to feel her stomach tighten.

"Oh Lord!" she thought, "What must I look like?" Bereft of Mark's umbrella (and the forethought of sensible clothing) Sarah had got very wet, very quickly and was now standing, arms spread limply in protest at being doused. Feigning composure, she made an attempt to redeem herself. "Lurk here often?"

He laughed. "Only when it's raining."

"Me too" she shrugged. Their eyes met.

"That's what comes of habit." He smiled as he said it; a rich, languorous smile that poured from his mouth into his eyes until they too, were brimming over.

Sarah could not mistake its intent - nor could she escape it; his eyes travelled the length of her body, pinning her to the pavement.

"I've thought of you all afternoon – I simply couldn't get you out of my head."

"Oh, I'm sorry." Sarah wasn't sure whether to be flattered or apologetic.

"Don't be sorry!" he laughed, moving closer to her, "Just make it up to me!"

"I'm not sure what you mean" she lied.

"Then let me show you."

It took him less than a second to find her in the darkness. Before she knew it, his mouth was on hers and she could not help but return the long, deep kiss into which she had been forced. He tasted like peppermint, reminding her strangely of Tic-tacs – and his lips were soft and surprisingly cold. 'Did he know I'd come this way?' she thought, 'has he been waiting for me?' Amidst the gale of questions and confused thought, Sarah heard him urging her to submit.

"Give in" he growled, his voice so gruff that Sarah shuddered.

"Let everything go – and give in."

So she did. His hands on her buttocks, he guided her deftly into the alcove from which he had materialised and pressed her hard against the wall, tugging her jacket from her shoulders so that she was bound by it at the elbows, her arms forced to her side. Sarah felt the damp brick through her shirt and then his tongue on her neck and his fingers at her collar, travelling down towards the buttons. What if they were seen? Sarah felt that she should say something, a rebuttal, or rebuke, something in defence of herself. But she said nothing. She was frightened that a single word from her would stop him – and she didn't want to stop him. Sarah knew that she wanted this; more anything else in the world, she wanted to feel alive. They made love right there, beneath the bridge, hidden within an alcove that formed the entrance to one of its many long abandoned arches. Every few minutes, trains packed tightly with commuters would trundle over them and the bridge would shudder its response, grumbling wordlessly at the caravan of over laden carriages rambling along its spine.

After it was over, they giggled; their fifteen minutes of passion suddenly seeming ridiculous. The rain had stopped and the street seemed suspended in that stunned sparseness that always follows a downpour.

"I hope you know I'm a married woman – well, almost!" she said hoarsely, avoiding eye contact as she pushed her skirt down over her hips, smoothing out the wrinkles with her palms.

"Me too" he laughed, it was a splendid, husky laugh, " – almost!"

The moment arrived without warning, like an unwelcome visitor. Sarah hit earth.

"Well, I... mm, need to get cigarettes, so I'm uh, heading this way." she pointed in the direction from which she came.

In response, he stabbed the air over his shoulder with his thumb. "I'm that way."

Sarah feigned indifference and flicked the hair away from her eyes with the back of her hand. "Well then, see you around."

"Yeah, see you around" he said and bestowed on her one last brilliant smile before departing. She watched him turn the corner onto Union Street, his unbuttoned raincoat caught by the wind like a cape, flashing its plaid crimson lining.

Now she really needed a cigarette.

The first thing Sarah heard as she opened the front door was the tickety-tap of Mark on the computer. She pulled off her jacket and hung it on the coat rack only to discover it had brick dust and dirt stains all over the sleeves. Sarah allowed herself a wry smile and then took the jacket, with the shopping she had bought, into the kitchen where she rolled it up and tucked it inside the washing machine. "I'd better get that washed tonight" she thought.

"Sarah, is that you?" she heard Mark call.

"Yes, it's me" she called back and followed her voice into the study.

Mark looked up from the computer. "You're late. Had a good day?"

"Yes, very good thank you. I met up with an old friend on the way home and…"

Sarah wasn't sure of the best way to phrase it. "And, uh, stopped to catch up."

She felt herself flush and strode briskly across to the window, affecting a curiosity in the weather. "It poured it down, did you notice?"

Mark's gaze had followed her across the room and now he studied her, with an amused, thoughtful expression. "Yes, couldn't miss it. You look great wet by the way."

Sarah turned sharply. "Do I?"

"Yes, very."

"Well that's handy because I am – very!"

They both smiled, holding one another's gaze, each searching the face of the other.

Sarah could feel the colour creeping up around her throat. "Any ideas for dinner?" she demanded cheerfully.

"Yes, we're going out. I've booked a table at Nuno's."

Sarah moved towards the door, "Fantastic! I'll go get ready."

"Yes, you do that. We'll drive, it's cosier."

He'd turned back to the computer, his fingers, once again, pecking frantically at the keyboard (it always reminded Sarah a little of greedy birds and she often had teased him about it).

She stepped back into the hall way and immediately noticed his raincoat laying crumpled on the floor, its garish tartan lining glaring up at her. When she picked it up, the carpet underneath was sodden and the coat hung damp and heavy in her hand. Sarah brought it to her nose and inhaled the smell of rain and brick dust - and Mark. She smiled; it was a tight-lipped, lop sided smile, full of lust and reminiscence.

Once sated by its scent, ensured forever of the memory it would bring her, she shook the coat gently and hung it on the coat rack, where her jacket had briefly sat.

The Vase

"Oh for God's sake, what a foul, filthy, disgusting, repugnant, vile…" Running out of adjectives Clara decided to throw the door keys with appropriate venom on to the rather ugly maple telephone stand Jack's mother had bought them, half hoping they would scratch it (and half hoping they wouldn't. It was, after all, worth a fair bit of money). She stomped into the kitchen to put away the shopping she'd just bought and rediscovered her vocabulary with a string of expletives. Two of the three laminate worktops had been converted into collages comprised of solidified gunk suspiciously resembling peanut butter and cream cheese. The third boasted the entire contents of their crockery cupboard in the putrid condition that, as Jack had a wont to quip when questioned, were in fact 'cunningly disguised Petri dishes'. If she heard that one again tonight there would be trouble.

Every time Clara went away for work, even if it was only overnight, somehow Jack managed to convert their normally organised and relatively clean one bedroom Hampstead flat into a despicable hovel. How her boyfriend managed to disperse his used shirts, socks and boxer shorts throughout every room so effectively eluded Clara. "He must literally shed them as he walks, like some form of lizard." She pondered aloud. The metaphor pleased her. Suddenly she envisaged Jack's trademark cotton boxers slipping from those dark, muscular hips and coming to rest about his ankles as he stood over the boiling kettle, spooning sugar into an awaiting coffee cup. In spite of her annoyance, Clara smiled lasciviously. He'd be home soon. The clock on the oven read five-fifteen; she had an hour. Clara knew that, as much as she dearly wished to be the kind of woman who could plonk herself down on the sofa amidst the debris and watch a bit of telly, unflustered by the pungent memoirs of Saturday's football game emanating from the kitbag still wedged beneath the coffee table, she wasn't and couldn't.

Marks and Spencer's packet meals stored neatly in two piles in the fridge (there was no way she was cooking first night home and there was fat chance of him doing it) Clara took a deep breath and ventured into the living room. As predicted, the kitbag was indeed beneath the coffee table propagating new species of bacteria; its uncanny base note mingling with Monday's work socks, exact whereabouts unknown and probably still sodden from beloved's journey home through the rain. (Clara recalled their phone call of the previous evening. Although warm and dry in Paris where the shoot had been held, in London, the rain had been torrential.)

"Thanks my love." She muttered and did what she knew she must with the requisite amount of dread: sniff out the abandoned footwear so that she may repatriate them to the laundry basket in the bathroom.

Several disgusted grunts and groans later, with all offending items re-housed in their fit and proper place, Clara cast an appreciative eye over her once more tidy home. Decorating the carpet in front of the sofa was an assembly of crumbs where Jack had obviously dined on crackers at some point in the previous three days that constituted Clara's absence. With a sigh she carried the stash of cups, saucers and sticky glassware she had collected into the kitchen with the intention of ordering Jack to stack the dishwasher when he got in, and then poked her head inside the dark, cluttered space that was their hallway cupboard and home to Henry, the vacuum cleaner.

As if it were a giant squid, Clara wrestled with the hefty red tub and its one concertinaed black tendril, dragging the unwilling creature into the living room. The eponymous Henry was a cumbersome, clumsy thing but Clara was fond of it, if only for the fact that it had a sort of sentimental value. It was almost four years ago that she and Jack had stumbled upon one another, their eyes meeting over a display unit laden with various cleaning equipment in the domestic goods department of John Lewis. Henry's banal and now peeling smiley face had been the mutual focus of their attention.

"How auspicious," Clara had thought at the time, as they had sat chatting over a pot of tea and two stale uneaten Eccles Cakes in the store's cafeteria, "A man who actually vacuums." It wasn't until three dates later that Jack made his confession. It turned out that he had actually been there with the intention of treating himself to a new PlayStation but having entered the lift on the ground floor and spied Clara's voluptuous bottom in its mirrored walls and become entranced by the tight, chocolate coloured curls that, in those days, had danced carelessly across her shoulders, Jack had never made it to audio-visuals. Instead he had followed her at a discrete distance through kitchenware, soft furnishings and into the domestic hardware department, calculating the right moment to make his move. Henry had simply been part of his tactic. Given the infancy of their relationship, the confession, although obviously embarrassing for Jack, proved fruitful. Deeply flattered that anyone should think her of worthy of such pursuit (and the purchase of an unwanted, stupidly overpriced vacuum cleaner) Clara had slept with him that very same night. Three months later they had found the flat in Hampstead, complete with wall-to-wall carpeting, and moved in together. Henry, having finally been given a purpose in life other than as a tool of deception, moved in with them.

"I went to John Lewis a reckless boy," Jack would later laugh during dinner parties as he recounted the anecdote, "And came out a domesticated man."

Clara was dubious as to the latter statement but didn't quibble having been given the illustrious role of providing the punch line. "It wouldn't have been so bad except for the fact that the studio flat Jack was living in had only laminated wood flooring!"

Their dinner companions would titter appreciatively and Jack and Clara would clasp hands, smiling beatifically at one another. It was their party piece, "Look at us, so much in love."

And they were, Clara thought fondly as, one by one, she plucked the ornaments from the book shelves beside the window and gave each a once over with her 'magic' yellow dust-grabbing cloth. Despite the inevitable ups and downs, they were still in love, she told herself. She'd known from the outset that she'd made the right choice. Funny, warm, clever... okay, a bit of a slob (hmm, actually a massive slob when it came to domestic hygiene) but his personal cleanliness she couldn't fault. Never had she known a man spend so much time in the bathroom; nor did she know what it was that he did in there – Jack kept the door resolutely shut, thankfully. Not that she had boundary issues or anything, just a healthy dislike of brushing her teeth to the discordant strains of her boyfriend emptying his bowels. Holding a little porcelain owl up to the light to check for residual dust, she smirked at the unintended pun and turned to glance at the carriage clock over the fireplace; six o'clock, he wouldn't be long now.

On the windowsill stood a small blue china vase; it was always the last thing she picked up when she dusted - reluctantly, as if touching it would bring her bad luck. She let her index finger trace the pattern of barely discernable fissures across the delicate curve of its body. They spread like a venous web from the vase's rim to its base. The broken pieces had remained unmentioned on the windowsill for months, and what had once been a hand painted motif of a blue silhouetted Chinese farmer following a blue ox across a blue field under a blue cloud filled sky, bordered top and bottom by swirling blue flowers had lain fractured and forlorn on a piece of kitchen towel, slithers of a world waiting to be reconstructed. Finally, in a moment of heightened guilt or regret, Jack had spent several hours gluing it back together in the belief that his mending the vase would absolve him of his sins against her. It hadn't. Small blue world intact, the cracks were still visible and the vase would never again be that perfect keepsake that Clara had so loved.

They had been living together for just over two years when Clara had come home one day to find Jack sitting on the sofa in the darkened living room, his head in his hands, the flat unusually silent.

"Hey Mr Mope, what on earth are you doing?" she had asked, laughing at the sombre expression that greeted her.

"Thinking."

Clara had sat beside him, waiting patiently for Jack to continue, his gaze fixed upon the slumbering thirty-six inch plasma screen filling the maw that was once an open fireplace. A minute or more passed.

"This isn't working." he'd said finally.

Clara's eyes had swivelled to the TV. The remote sat on the stand beside it. "Really? What's wrong with it?"

"Everything." His head had dropped back into his hands. "I'm sorry."

It had taken Clara a couple of seconds to realise that it wasn't the television Jack was referring to – and another second or two before the wave of dread had immersed her, filling her lungs with thick, cloying fear.

Feeling herself reel backwards, Clara's neatly manicured fingernails clung grimly to the leather beneath her. Her mouth had moved, words had formed, but all she'd heard was a tiny little voice that didn't belong to her.

"Oh." it had said. "Sorry."

Clara stroked the vase gently with the duster in her hand, trying to remember what Jack had said next. She cringed now to think of it: how stupid she must have looked, waiting for his response, perched beside him like an innocently adoring puppy that had just been kicked, still searching the face it loved for approval. Two years of numb denial had softened the memory of that sharp pain in her chest to a stubborn, lingering ache, but the dour taste of shame that came with it had never faded. He had packed some of his clothes that night and left to stay with a friend; Clara had never found out whom – she had never asked. Instead she had wandered about the flat, eating cornflakes out of the box, picking up the remnants of him: tightly wrapped balls of unwashed socks he'd tossed into corners of their bedroom, CDs he'd left scattered around the stereo - each thoughtlessly strewn item evidence of his continuing untidy existence in her life. The strangest thing was that Clara could not remember an argument; there must have been one. Would she, as vociferous as she was, have let the man she loved so desperately just pick up his car keys and go without any type of a battle? It seemed unlikely and yet all she remembered was the sensation of childlike helplessness once he had gone, the dull recognition that a decision had been made for her – about her. Then the repetitive murmur of demons had materialized and followed her from room to room, whispering repeatedly that she was unloved, unwanted. Finally she had drowned out their chatter with a bottle of sour red wine.

Holding the vase now in her hands, tracing the scars through its delicate pattern, Clara tried to recall the moment she had hurled it at the wall opposite. Had he been there? Had she thrown it at him? She liked to think she had; but of all the memories she had buried, she knew that this was not one. Although in the fading light she could not see it, somewhere along its plaster expanse Clara knew an indentation remained. Like the vase, the wall still bore the wounds that she herself had hidden.

Jack had called the next day. It was a Saturday; that she remembered, as she had spent the day curled up on the sofa watching dull black and white movies containing flurries of sword fighting and open shirted knights with pencil thin moustaches and effeminate bobs. Replete with apologetic declarations of temporary madness, the phone call had been melodramatic and Jack had arrived back at the flat an hour later and pulled her into his arms. Clara recalled crying copiously, drenching his T-shirt with angry tears. Still, she remembered nothing of what she had said – or the vase. They must have talked, re-negotiated their alliance in some fashion or another as he had spent that night in bed beside her, splayed like a skydiver and snoring throatily. Clara still had the image in her head; she had sat up watching him by the harsh orange glow of the streetlight that invaded their bedroom when the curtains weren't fully drawn. Even now it galled her that during those long miserable hours in which she'd kept vigil, the fury that had initially consumed Clara had retreated from the room as humbly as the darkness, skewered by dawn's light and her own fervent gratitude for his return.

The apologies had continued for another day or so and then been replaced with a brazen complacency. By midweek, Jack had begun referring to his departure the previous week as a 'hiccup'. Clara had learned to loathe that word and its portentous new meaning. When Jack had had another bout of 'hiccups' a month later, Clara had vowed never to let him return; a threat that lasted no longer than a fortnight. Suddenly she remembered; that was when she had thrown the vase! This time he had called her from work, almost nonchalant, as if he were cancelling a subscription to a magazine. Clara had been stuck at home for a couple of weeks having finally given up her hairdressing job at Vidal Sassoon's and gone self-employed a few months earlier. It had been a struggle to find regular assignments without the benefit of industry contacts but she'd been determined to go it alone after spending almost a decade kowtowing to one pedantic salon manager after another. A series of unsuccessful interviews had taken its toll on her confidence and Clara had begun to feel the prickliness of depression creeping under her skin. Jack had been so supportive, reassuring her that he could easily afford to pay the rent on the flat for a while, and had even come home one day with a beautiful A4 leather valise for her to put her portfolio shots in. He had been so caring, so effusive in his belief in her the last thing Clara had expected was a repetition of his earlier desertion – particularly not over the telephone. Even now, the banality of it made her shudder. Again Jack had used the words, "I'm sorry, this isn't working." On this occasion she'd known instantly what he was talking about. Again, he had collected his clothes, and this time his CDs as well; even the dozen or so books he owned (those trashy thrillers he insisted on reading) were gathered from the shelves and sifted through – those he rejected left discarded on the sofa. Clara had stood in the doorway, watching, knowing that it would be she that would move them later. Jack had appeared more resolute than before as he moved quietly around the flat, stuffing things into a large sports bag that Clara had never seen and could only assume had been bought especially – and when that was full, into the black bin bags that Clara kept under the sink. She remembered watching him unravel them one at a time, tearing each from the roll with an angry calmness that had confused her. What on earth had he to be angry about? She had asked him "Why Jack?" again and again, as she had followed him from room to room. It wasn't as if she'd been unfaithful; "What is it Jack? What have I done?"

The repetition had seemed to annoy him further and embarrassed Clara, who suffered his disdainful silence like a neglected child, weeping openly. His belongings piled outside in the communal hallway, beyond the flat's front door, Jack had finally turned towards her and paused just long enough for Clara to see the pain in his face.

"I do love you Clara," he had whispered hoarsely, "But I'm not sure I love you enough."

She'd rather he had slapped her; she certainly wished that she had slapped him. Instead she had laughed, a small half laugh, half snort, and rolled her eyes as if to say 'how ridiculous', whilst inside she'd swooned and desperately willed her knees to remain locked a little longer, wondering how she could fold to the floor without appearing pathetic. Relieved by Clara's bravado, Jack had dropped his gaze in a show of deference and quickly pulled the front door shut behind him. Sliding down the wall, Clara had listened to the rustle of plastic being dragged down two flights of stairs, counting the bumps between landings. Too shocked to speak, to call after him, to ask what it was he didn't love her enough to do, Clara had collected her breath and staggered over to the window to watch Jack load the car and drive away.

The light was fading now, the vase's pattern fading with it. Still seated on the sofa, Clara scanned the opposite wall. "How dare he?" she thought. "How dare he come back again? How dare I let him?"

As Jack had driven away with half her world tipped onto the back seat of his car, leaving her once more alone and utterly confused as to why, is that when she'd done it? Had she plucked the vase from the windowsill and hurled it at the mirror that once hung there, watching both it and her shatter in unison?

She'd forgotten about the mirror. It'd had been a cheap one they'd bought in Camden Market shortly after moving in. Later, finding the frame wedged behind a stepladder in the hallway cupboard, Jack had joked about the ensuing seven years' bad luck Clara had paid little attention: she wasn't particularly superstitious and considered Jack's raising the subject to be in poor taste. The vase, however, had been a different matter entirely and had made her feel wretched. Clara stared dolefully down at the diminutive object in her hands; a birthday gift from her father the year he had died, it was all she really had left of him. Sure, Jack had super-glued the thing together so that it could impersonate what it once was, but the vase was useless now: it would never again hold water. Repairing it had been a futile gesture. How could Jack have expected her to believe that it would be as strong as its former self?

He had come back to her two weeks later, full of apologies once more. Defeated and vulnerable, Clara had taken him back with little protest. Her cheeks burned hot to think of it now. Back in their bed, Jack had beseeched her not to speak of it, to forget it had happened. "A foolish, foolish mistake," he had called it. Again he had used the word hiccup. "Let's put it behind us - move on." And with that he had silenced her, stolen her right to rebuke. In a belated realisation, the brutality of what he had done swam through Clara, making her nauseous. As though she'd had no choice he had cajoled her into believing that it was the better part of herself who would rise above his transgressions – that her magnanimity made her somehow victorious. Assuming absolution was inevitable, even his apologies had shown no humility.

She studied the vase's tranquil scene, no longer perfect, and imagined herself being led by the ox, pushing the plough across the field, threading the flowers through its border. She longed to step into the blue and wade through its shallow glaze, but all she saw were the cracks - that's all she would ever see. Suddenly she heard the front door slam and her heart lurched miserably.

"Clara, are you here?"

Clara said nothing, feeling the timbre of his voice filling the air with masculine energy. Jack entered the room, dumping his coat over a chair. He sounded breathless and had obviously taken the stairs two at a time – something he often did when in a hurry to get home. When he saw her his frown unfolded into a broad, even-toothed white grin that made him look impossibly handsome.

"There you are. I've missed you!"

As though it were a baby, wrapping her arms around the delicate piece of china that would never again be a keepsake, Clara emitted a slow, acquiescent sigh before answering. She really had loved it so.

"Hey sweetie, it's dark in here. What are you doing?"

Jack stood over Clara, his face frozen in curiosity, awaiting her reply.

Unnoticed in the gloom, a tear rolled down Clara's cheek.

"Thinking." she responded softly.

A Quick Lunch

They were absolutely fantastic – possibly the sexiest things she'd ever seen. Shading her eyes with one hand and trying not to let her breath fog up the glass, Anna peered at them longingly, noting the delicate vine imprint edging the cowboy-cut cuffs. It had been a long time since she had owned a pair of knee length leather boots but knew only too well what effect such things had on a girl's confidence – and, unfortunately, her wallet. The price tag, propped innocently against the toes' pointed tips, was inscribed with three figures; no decimal point, just a copperplate pound sign, the solitary number three and two defiant nines glaring back at her. At that moment her pocket began to vibrate and above the sounds of the street Anna heard the faint synthetic strains of her mobile's ring tone. She reached for it, grateful of the distraction.

"Hello." she said, pressing the handset to her ear.

"Anna, how did it go at the florist?" It was Kerry, her best friend and soon to be bridesmaid.

"It was okay. I think I've made a decision."

"You don't sound very excited," said her friend. "I thought choosing the flowers was supposed to be the best bit."

Anna sighed. "Oh it was fine. It's just that I'm stood in front of Aldo's on Oxford Street looking at the most gorgeous boots in the world!"

Kerry laughed. "What's the problem then? Buy them!"

"The problem is the price tag. Honestly Kerry, it's criminal!"

"How criminal?"

"Let me put it this way, either I can walk up the aisle of a church full of flowers, holding a bouquet of lilies with you and Tracey at my heel looking splendid in baby's breath diadems…"

"Diadems?" her friend snorted. "What the hell is a…"

"Headbands with little flowers on them. Don't worry it's not definite. Anyway, it's a matter of boots or flowers! Under the circumstances I think the flowers win." There was a short silence on the other end. "Kerry? Are you there?"

"Yes, sorry, just trying to flag down a cab. I'm late for work – again! I tell you what girl; I'm willing to sacrifice the headband. In fact, I say stuff the flowers, who needs a bouquet, just wear the boots!"

Anna laughed, her friend's sanguine wit acting like a much needed tonic. "Nice idea sweetie, but it wouldn't really work, I'd have to swap the veil for a Stetson. Hell Kerry, I am so disorganised. This is turning into a shambles!"

Anna was starting to feel overwhelmed by the amount of planning left to do before the wedding. It was less than two months away and she hadn't even ordered the wedding cake, arranged for a DJ or made the obligatory gesture of a 'social' visit with the vicar who was marrying them (although that wasn't her fault; she couldn't go alone, they had to visit as a couple and so far Nat had been very awkward in the matter of setting a definite visiting date). Anna's voice grew morose. "I thought this was supposed to be exciting."

"Well isn't it?" asked Kerry.

"No. No it isn't – just exhausting."

Sensing that it was not a topic on which to linger, her friend deftly changed the subject. "What are you doing in town today? Don't you normally work on Tuesday?"

"I do but I'm playing truant. I needed to sort out the flowers before Friday; the woman gave me a deadline. I don't know why they're so tight about it, they're only flowers!"

"Well, it's done now. Are you going back to work?" Kerry asked.

"No way! Nat's office is just near here so I thought I'd nip in and drag him out to lunch. The poor guy never leaves his desk, just sits there with a sandwich that he buys on the way in every morning. I do feel sorry for him Kerry, he's got so much work on right now, he's never home before ten."

Her friend snorted with derision. "Don't Anna! He's left you to organise this wedding all on your own. No wonder you're exhausted! Your dad's footing the bill for most of this so why the extra hours?"

Anna felt a lecture coming on; she didn't need it. She'd asked both herself and Nat that question several times and was still none the wiser. When confronted, Nat had barked about keeping in line for promotion and *'the corporate expectations of a man in his position'*, but not once had he given her a straight answer. Tired of being the bad guy eventually Anna had given up and resigned herself to planning the wedding alone.

"Men are just not good at these things, you know that," she told Kerry. "Listen, I have to go if I'm going to get Nat out of the office long enough to have lunch. I'll ring you tonight."

"Okay. Are you far enough away from those boots yet?"

Anna chuckled, recalling the start of their conversation. She hadn't actually moved from where she'd being standing, but now, allowing herself one last glance at the sumptuous leather creations on display, manoeuvred her way between other dawdling window shoppers and slipped down the nearest side street. "Boot crisis over!" she declared and swapped cheery goodbyes with her friend before tucking the mobile back in her pocket.

Working as a receptionist in a North London Medical Practice, Anna rarely came into the centre of town. She would have preferred to use a local florist for the wedding flowers but the best quote had, to her surprise, come from a small florist's shop in Victoria. On a whim she had called in sick, caught the train to Victoria station and had finished at the florist's by half past ten, leaving her the rest of the day to wander amongst the crowds of Oxford Street in search of a pair of shoes to match the pale blue going-away suit she'd bought for the reception. Anna didn't like the west-end, finding no charm in the grotty and confusing myriad of alleyways that filtered office workers from one crammed street to another; the mannequin-stuffed facades of Regent Street she saw as an annual necessity, tolerated only during Spring sales and the weeks leading up to Christmas. Anna pulled at her collar wishing she were in the comfortably heated shopping centre a half mile from her home where the car park, toilets, coffee shop and supermarket were all just an escalator's ride away from each other. "That's the way to shop!" she mused, stepping between the few puddles remaining from yesterday's rain.

Having walked the length of the unknown road onto which she'd turned, Anna found herself on Poland Street. "Hallelujah! I've emerged somewhere vaguely familiar." she thought thankfully.

The design house in which Nat worked as an art director wasn't far away. It had been a long time since she'd last surprised Nat at work and the thought of a pleasant lunch with him made Anna smile. They hadn't spent any quality time together in ages so she was sure he'd be happy to see her. (She made a mental note not to mention the flowers or the DJ – or the vicar; every time she had tried to discuss the wedding recently they had started to quarrel.) Anna looked at her watch; it was one o'clock already. There were a couple of places on Beak Street she knew of that did good, quick food but most of them were Chinese buffets and Anna fancied Italian food (Nat loved pasta so she knew there would be no debate on that score).

As she scoured the area for landmarks that would lead her to Nat's office, Anna's gaze fell upon a quaint green awning with the name *Santorini* splashed cross it. It looked perfect and, although still a few streets away from the design house and now running out of time, Anna decided to cross over and scan the menu; Nat would have a fit if it turned out she'd unwittingly dragged him somewhere expensive for what would undoubtedly be a rushed forty-minute lunch.

The prices on the menu, displayed in an ornate wooden cabinet beside the entrance were, much to Anna's delight, extremely reasonable. Wondering if it would be full at this hour of the day, she let her head fall to one side and her gaze bypass the cabinet, into the restaurant itself. Through the glass she saw crisp white napkins and unlit candles adorning every table; it looked lovely she decided, and some of the tables were empty, which was a good sign. As her eyes adjusted to the darkness within, Anna could make out a small party of men and women on one side and several couples on the other. She was about to pull away when she caught sight of one of the booths at the rear. Sat opposite a young blonde, with whom he held hands across the table, was a man in his thirties wearing a pale grey suit. The two dimly lit figures seemed deep in conversation and neither one looked happy. The man's head was down and his face turned away but still, Anna reasoned, he was the spitting image of Nat; not only did he look like her fiancé, the man's suit was identical to the one Anna had herself laid out for Nat that very morning.

"Now that is weird! Wait until I tell –" The realisation pierced Anna's chest like a paring knife, slicing through her with merciless accuracy and causing her lungs to contract with one sharp sob. At that moment the couple leaned towards each other and remained there in a lingering kiss. Anna could see clearly the profile of her soon to be husband and even make out the words he mouthed as he pulled away; *"I love you,"* he had said. Anna saw the girl smile - a puerile, coquettish smile that froze Anna's bones and made Nat laugh. The same three words were passed soundlessly back by the unknown blonde to her boyfriend – *her* boyfriend, Anna's boyfriend, the man *she* planned to marry. "Those words belong to me," a voice inside her raged. "They're mine!" For four years she and Nat had traded those words almost daily. Through happy summer holidays, as sticking plasters for arguments, after making love and over breakfast, those words had become for them a currency; they had a price tag, its value far beyond that of one white wedding – or so she had thought. It occurred to Anna that with those three stolen words, Nat had given away all that was precious to her. "How can that be?" she demanded aloud. "How can that be?" He had woken up next to her that morning, wrapped his arms around her sleepy form and tucked his face into the nape of her neck. "Good morning lovely." he had whispered - and then those same small three words Anna had thought she'd owned outright.

Anna gently lifted her fingertips, which had been pressed against the glass and watched numbly as their print faded, aware that as they evaporated so did her future; everything she had planned for, everything she'd been promised was suddenly gone. Resting their heads against each other the two conspirators looked so entwined and at peace that, peering at them through the glass like a thief, Anna felt as though she were the perpetrator - as if she were stealing from them their secret. Deceitful and unjust as it was, it was theirs, brought to life by a part of Nat Anna now realised she no longer possessed: the more tender, willing core of him that only new love invigorated.

Slowly, Anna drew away from the window, backing onto the pavement. Until that moment, she and Nat had been in love – or so she had thought. Perhaps their passion had morphed into something more solid and sustainable than lust, but Anna had believed that to be a good thing; treasuring the notion that, in the hours they were apart, each sat like a reassuring shadow on the other's shoulder. She'd read that in a poem somewhere and thought it beautiful. Now the sentiment seemed idiotic. "What a sham." she thought bitterly. "What a goddamn sham!"

There was an empty bench ten or so yards along the street and Anna slumped onto it not knowing what to do; there was so much noise from the traffic and passing voices that she couldn't think straight. The memory of the woman's coy smile flashed before her. "What kind of woman would do that?" she said aloud in disbelief, attracting a wary glance from a harried passer-by who in response, tucked his chin into his scarf and made his stride a little brisker. Then Anna remembered Nat's face, the kiss she had seen and the words he had spoken; he had looked like a man in love. She struggled to comprehend what that meant as the tears spilled freely across her cheeks and fell unchecked from her jaw, forming tiny dark stains on her dress. "And what kind of fool am I?" she questioned the pale sky above, conscious of the vast space around her in that small crowded street. "What kind of fool am I?"

It had begun to rain again and through her stupor, Anna could feel the tips of her fingers deaden. The bench's patterned iron frame felt cold against her back, she couldn't stay there. Flattening her palms on her lap, Anna contemplated her unpainted nails and the ellipse of skin on each knuckle. The solitaire diamond on her ring finger that Nat had bought eight months before twinkled mockingly back at her. They'd chosen it together: Nat not being the down on one knee kind of guy had suggested they 'get hitched' over breakfast one weekend. Thrilled, Anna had said yes without hesitation and they had driven into town that same afternoon to find a ring. It was a modest diamond, but what Anna had wanted, which was something simple and pretty to complement the wedding bands they intended to swap. Nat had made jokes with the young man behind the counter about retiring from the market and Anna, full of smiles and gratitude had laughed with them – graciously remaining mute when he'd referred to her as 'the impending ball and chain'.

Anna's collective memory of every thoughtless thing that Nat had ever said and done - a Pandora's box of small hurts, suddenly flew open, its tenuous lock no longer held fast by naivety and denial. Anna sifted through them, her gaze fixed on the ring, noting the precision of its nine-carat clasp and how the petite clear stone caught the light, defying its own pallid countenance with a wondrous reflection of colours. It was beautiful; she loved that ring in the same way she'd loved Nat: with a light heart – one of faith and optimism. Both had become icons of contentment to Anna with the image of her brighter, better self projected upon them. And then it occurred to her: there would be no flowers, no veil, no vows to write for the vicar – and no wedding band to join this ring. And then something else occurred to her. Anna checked her watch; it was now twenty past one. She would have to be quick.

Anna got back to the restaurant a little before two. Instinct told her they would still be there and she did not pause to peer into the window as she had before but opened the heavy glass door and stepped straight in. The restaurant's warmth hit her immediately and she paused for a second to enjoy it, letting her eyes adjust to the dimly lit room. A waiter began to saunter towards her but Anna waved him away with a wordless smile, pointing to the table where Nat and the woman still sat drinking coffee, engrossed in conversation.
"I am trying, I really am." Anna heard Nat say pleadingly as she strode towards them.
"It isn't good enough Nathan." the woman responded. "This isn't fair on me!"
"Or me!" Anna added, now standing before them, her gazing resting on Nat.
The mercurial swivel of his head reminded Anna of the American eagle they had seen during a visit to London zoo the previous summer. She had felt sorry for the caged creature perched on a low branch returning their stare - its eyes blinking at her rapidly as Nat's did now. Her fiancé, however, was not having the same effect
"Anna!" he cried, his expression, a blend of incredulity and horror.
"Nathan!" she responded brightly, flashing him a broad, albeit taut, smile. "And this is?" she added, her grin shifting to the blonde beside him.
By way of response, the blonde shuffled awkwardly and then lifted her chin to look Anna in the eye.
"Ella." she said.

"Nice." The word bled through Anna's lips like the hiss of a snake but the tone was sweet – airy even. It had its desired effect, the woman's eyebrows shot up in confusion. But Anna didn't care; with the sibilance of the 'c' still on her lips, she had thrown her gaze back to Nat, who was staring up at her like a wide-eyed infant.

"Anna listen, we need to talk…"

"No Nathan." The name felt strange in her mouth, she had never called him that. "No. We don't need to talk." Reaching into a side pocket Anna pulled out a hastily folded slip of white paper and tossed it onto the table.

"What's that?" Nat asked her.

"I thought you should have it," she answered smoothly, her gaze fixed upon him with as much innocence as she could muster. "You did pay for it after all, and I always said I'd give it back. Although…" Anna mocked a giggle, "I only said that because I never thought I'd have to. What a mug eh? Anyway, a girl's got to stick to her word."

Nat picked up the crumpled piece of paper, unfolding it slowly. Both Anna and the blonde watched quietly as he scanned its contents, his expression morphing from that of fear to one of utter confusion.

"It's a pawn ticket," he mumbled. "What for?"

"The ring, Nathan. The engagement ring."

Nat's head shot up, his back straightening instantly to a self-righteous stance.

"I paid £600 for that!" He objected, his face ruddy with shame and annoyance.

Anna's smile tightened. "Well, now you can pay for it all over again!"

"Good to finally meet you Ella." she chirped brightly as she nodded a farewell to them both and turned away.

With the weight of their gaze on her back, Anna strode out of the restaurant as poised as her trembling frame would allow. Only once she'd reached the bench where she'd sat less than an hour earlier, mortified and numb, did Anna stop to breathe. She wasn't really sure what to do next – or where to go; she could go home of course, but then what had she to do there but pack?

"No," she thought. "I can't go home. Not yet."

Behind her eyes the tears waited for their cue to spill over, and then a pinch at her ankle caused her to glance down. As she did she smiled; they were a little tight in the toe she realised, but she knew the leather would give quickly - Italian leather usually did.

"That's it!" Anna said aloud, knowing now what she would do. "I shall simply walk for a while."

Stepping off the curb, Anna paused to let a car to pass and then crossed the street. Despite the rain, it seemed a good day for a stroll. "After all," she reasoned, "I am wearing the most sensational pair of new boots!"

To the New Year

As was his habit, Derek strolled the length of the park and back before stopping to rest at his favourite bench opposite the emus' enclosure (third on the right when facing north). This particular bench was one of the very few scattered about the park which bore commemorative plaques; in this case, a small brass rectangle with the name Jessica Swinfen engraved upon it. Beneath the name were the words *Fruitstock organiser. Extraordinary woman. Very curly hair.* Derek thought it an unusual tribute, but liked the pragmatism of the two descriptions and felt that they somehow lent weight to the single compliment sandwiched between them. He wondered if this too were Ms Swinfen's favourite bench (surmising that Ms was probably the most appropriate title for the deceased, whose inscription gave no clue to her marital status). Perhaps it was the bench's vantage point of the zoo that had drawn her to it - as it had him. Derek was fond of London zoo, and always enjoyed his walks through Regents Park, particularly on quiet days like today. Most of all, he liked the emus. It was certainly a chilly afternoon however, and he wondered if the poor creatures felt the cold as they rustled back and forth along the perimeter fence of their small compound, tussling their feathered skirts like bedraggled cheerleaders. January the first, just another day he reasoned. Still, he could taste that faint tang of potential in the air, even in this perennially constant place. Derek felt he knew a thing or two about potential. Potential was a constant companion to many men - and women, of course. It was potential's bedfellow, fruition, which proved to be the more elusive – in Derek's experience at least.

One thing that could be counted on was the passage of time. It would be dark soon. Derek did not mind this eager stealth of the sun in the winter months; in fact it was sometimes convenient. "The shortening of a day is not always a bad thing," he muttered aloud, thinking of his home in Camden Square and those late summer evenings that lured children out onto the street, yelping and cursing outside his window till all hours of the night.

Derek took a small chrome flask from the side pocket of his overcoat and, using its cap as a cup, poured himself some tea laced with rum – a favourite tipple of his father's, God rest his soul. The flask had been a complimentary gift with a stationary order he had placed at work. No one else had wanted it (he'd been sure to enquire, thinking it only fair, as the flask was, after all, rightfully company property) and so Derek had taken it home with him, knowing it would be of use on just this type of occasion.

A couple strolled past him, each with a floppy arm encircling the other's waist - the way young lovers seemed to do these days. What ever happened to holding hands? He wondered. Far more dignified than dangling from each other, limbs entwined like capuchin monkeys. He caught snatches of their conversation as they passed: the young chap's confessions of drunkenness the night before and her New Year resolutions. (Something to do with chocolate and a treadmill at the gym with her name on it.) Derek imagined that the majority of Britain would be doing the same right now: spilling over with hazy regret and empty promises whilst nursing the remains of the hangover they have earned from their bacchanalian exploits the night before.

There were several people scattered about the field behind him. Two teenagers playing football and another young couple with a little girl in tow, trailing after their dogs, their weary calls to heel ignored by both dogs and child. Unlike the toddler's spiteful rebellion, it appeared to Derek that the animals were simply lost in their own world, intent on tracing each other's scents and play fighting with other errant pets. The diversity of breeds never ceased to amaze Derek, who was baffled by the pocket size variety of miniature canines peering out of women's shoulder bags in those glossy magazines he scanned whilst waiting for the dentist. What on earth possessed these women to carry animals around likes dolls, stuffing the poor creatures into a pouch beside their mobile phone? Derek didn't understand the young women of today - nor the lads for that matter. The girls with their androgynous frames and the boys, well; he simply couldn't understand why they chose to wear their denim jeans unbelted and barely covering the hem of their boxer shorts – or indeed those sombre hoods that gave them the same odious facade as the grim reaper. Actually, the hooded youths' resemblance to Franciscan monks had occurred to him first, but Derek simply could not marry the image of men of the cloth shoving each other boisterously whilst barking expletives. Then again, nor could he envisage the grim reaper escorting some unfortunate soul into the afterlife with the words "Gotta admit it man, you well deserved that 'cos you're a wanker, innit?"

His rumination was abruptly cut short by the rasping pant of a muddy pawed but otherwise white Scottish terrier sniffing at his shoes. Derek regarded the little dog for a moment as it attempted to polish his stiff brown lace ups with a lipstick pink tongue. Suddenly Derek heard the name Peggy being called, each shrill syllable a separate note ringing through the still air. Further along the path stood a woman holding a leash, looking frantically about her. Derek noted the plumpness of her body beneath the taut woollen coat, and the way her chestnut coloured hair lifted away from her forehead, twisting back onto its self in loose curls that framed a wide pleasant face with flushed cheeks. As if feeling his stare, she turned, catching sight of both Derek and the dog. Spreading her arms in mock exasperation, she strode hurriedly towards him. Derek nodded in understanding and leant down to take hold of the inquisitive animal's collar. The dog, realising instinctively that its liberty was about to be curtailed, scurried away from him, circling his would be captor warily. By now, the woman was just a few feet away.

"You bad dog! Honestly," she huffed, throwing an apologetic smile in Derek's direction. "Peggy can be awfully nosey. She picks up the scent of something and she's off!"

Derek nodded awkwardly.

"Do you have a dog?"

"Sorry? Uh, no." As Derek 's eyes now met hers fully for the first time he was struck dumb for a second by the depth of her gaze. Her sapphire stare was illuminated further by the wide ingenuous smile she proffered. Derek found himself mumbling inanely.

"Don't mind me!" she piped brightly as she plonked her pneumatic frame down on the bench. "I've been running around after this naughty girl for half an hour!" She gestured towards the terrier, which came towards her with its head bowed humbly. The woman leant forward and rubbed the animal's ears briskly with both hands. "What are you? Yes, you're a cheeky girl!"

Derek sat uncomfortably beside her; not knowing whether it would be better to get up and leave or guide the woman's ramblings into some semblance of a conversation. He decided the most appropriate thing would be to wait to see if she addressed him once more.

"Funny that. She must smell something on you." The woman turned her whole body towards him quickly, declaring her deduction triumphantly. "Aha, a cat!"

"Uh, no, I'm afraid not."

The woman slumped at hearing Derek's response, seemingly crestfallen. "Oh. Thought I had it there."

"No. Sorry."

"Never mind," she shrugged, "Looks like we'll never know." And then she peeled off an ancient blue suede glove and held out her hand for Derek to shake. "My name is Mae."

Derek offered his hand in turn and the two of them laughed self-consciously, giving the encounter a sudden sense of formality. As she smiled again, Derek noticed how one of her front teeth stood just slightly askew of the other, considering it to be quite a charming imperfection.

"Just how long do you think that path is?" she gestured vaguely over her shoulder towards the park's main promenade. "It seems to go on forever!"

Derek smiled at her blitheness. "I believe you mean the Broad Walk. It is seven hundred metres start to finish." he replied. "Though of course that's not an exact figure."

At this, the painted lines that fashioned Mae's eyebrows shot up, forming two perfect arches. Like bridge supports, thought Derek. "Ooh, a man of numbers!" she exclaimed with delight. "I respect a man who knows his figures."

Derek acknowledged the compliment with an embarrassed nod.

Unabashed by his taciturn manner, Mae persisted. "I didn't catch your name."

"I didn't give it - sorry. My name is Derek"

He felt himself squirming a little beneath her gaze. Oblivious to her new acquaintance's discomfort, Mae continued to regard him as if she were sizing up a cut of beef for Sunday roast. "A doctor?" She ventured, and then shook her head emphatically. "No, no.

You've none of the airs and graces those lot carry with them." Mae placed a small pink hand on his arm. "I mean that in a good way."

Not wanting to interrupt her, Derek said nothing. He liked her inquisitiveness, her liveliness.

"Hmm, good with sums. A stockbroker!"

Derek hated to disappoint her, but he knew he must. "Nothing quite so adventurous. Just an accountant I'm afraid."

"Well fancy that!" She shrilled. "My uncle Harry was an accountant. Good man my uncle Harry - very clever."

"I haven't seen you in the park before. Do you come here often?" He'd spoken without thinking. As the words fell from his mouth, Derek cringed at the banality of the question they shaped. Mae didn't seen to mind.

"Have only been in the area for a week." She replied brightly. "Until recently I had a house in St John's Wood." She paused, her gaze shifting to the middle distance. "Downsizing I think they call it."

And Derek thought he saw her soft features melt into sadness for just a second as she scanned the undergrowth of the compound opposite for signs of life. He felt it time to assert himself.

"I'm afraid you've missed the Emus; they've have long since bedded down for the evening. I don't think they are too fond of the dark." He watched his own voice pull her back to earth.

"What? Oh." It took her a second to process his words. "Are there Emus? How marvellous." Mae caught sight of the flask and the cup Derek had been holding. "Ooh, that isn't tea is it?"

Derek nodded, "Would you like some? I must warn you that it has a little rum in it."

"All the better." Mae took the small cup between her palms, relishing the heat of the metal as he poured out more of the pungent milky brew.

Bringing it to her lips, she drained the vessel in one long draft then let out an appreciative sigh. "That was lovely." She said, handing back the cup. "Looks like I picked the right bench." And with that, she laughed, her eyes ablaze once more, warming Derek's body in a manner he had not experienced for years.

About the Author

Victoria Taylor Roberts was born under another name in West Yorkshire, England. In her early teens, her family moved to Sydney, Australia, where she was given a new name and a life to match. At the age of twenty, Victoria returned to England, chose yet another name for herself and settled in London where she remains to the present day. Oh yes – and she likes to write.

May 2012

Printed in Great Britain
by Amazon